WHERE DARKNESS CANNOT FOLLOW

A.M. DAYLIN

MOONCREST PUBLISHING

MOONCREST PUBLISHING

First published by Mooncrest Publishing 2024

This novel is entirely a work of fiction. The names, characters and incidents portrayed in it are the work of the author's imagination. Any resemblance to actual persons, living or dead, events or localities is entirely coincidental.

A.M. Daylin asserts the moral right to be identified as the author of this work.

First edition
ISBN (paperback): 979-8218396251
ISBN (hardcover): 979-8218441579
ISBN (ebook): 979-8218396275

Cover art by Benita Thompson
Editing by Hannah Gaudette
Proofreading by Brigitte Cromey
Typesetting by Benita Thompson

fully weaves in life lessons that are valuable for all ages. This book is a treasure trove for readers who love relatable characters, masterful writing, immersive prose, and an engaging plot. I know I won't be alone in staying up past my bedtime for this book."

—Hannah Gaudette,
author of the *Destined Duology*

"A. M. Daylin has created a heart-stopping story perfect for readers who want action without gore, angst without despair, and Christian themes without saccharine overtones. Effortlessly combining vivid world building, powerful themes, and complex characters who'll grab your heart from page one, *Where Darkness Cannot Follow* delivers a message straight to readers' hearts about their own worth and the power of being transformed by the Light. This is a story that has never failed to bring me to tears and is guaranteed to be enjoyed over and over in the years to come!"

—Brigitte Cromey,
author of *The Guardian's Oath*

*To anyone who has ever questioned
if they are enough.*

"ALL THE DARKNESS
IN THE WORLD CANNOT
EXTINGUISH THE LIGHT OF
A SINGLE CANDLE."

—*St. Francis of Assisi*

1

EZRO

"Ezro! Where you at, boy?"

My father's voice splinters through the cornfield like a strike of monsoon lightning. His thunderous steps halt at the edge of the crop before I hear swatted stalks rattling as he wades in. I hunker low in the shadows, bow held taut in my sunburned hand, breathing in the soil's rich aroma. I'm not sure why I think I'll get away with running, but I'll try anything before I surrender to Father taking me to Fen-fyre.

The rattling trades for a gentle rustle, soft as the first patters of rain—his broad shoulders brushing the limber leaves. His steps near with each nervous beat of my heart. A breeze tickles my nose. It teases of a storm to come, but I doubt it will be enough to stop Father today.

Today, he is the storm.

He shouts my name again, a whistle twittering through his fingers as if he's calling for a dog. Sometimes, I think that's all I am to him. Some dirty mutt my mother wanted so much that he caved. But Mother isn't alive to want me now, so I guess he's free to send me to my next master. *Grandfather.* The man responsible for forging my father into the weapon he is.

Think I'd rather be a stray.

"The carriage ain't gonna wait all day."

I sink lower beneath the green stalks. *Exactly what I'm hoping for.*

Below the leaves, I can see his holey boots stamping through the damp soil. His face enters my pocket of sight as he swipes the summer sweat off his brow with the back of his hand. He wipes it onto his pants with a bearish grumble. I miss all but the last of his complaints.

"…cost me extra makin' them wait."

Or cost you nothing if we just don't go.

I slip an arrow from my sewn leather quiver and nock it on the bow. The arrow's tip aims for him. Then, I slide it toward a stalk behind him, the furthest I can hit with a clean shot. The arrow launches, sneaking through the cornstalks with only the softest hiss and a wiggle of the leaves in its wake. It crashes with a loud jitter into my target. Father whips around, dashing toward my distraction. I stifle a laugh and bolt the other way. It won't do me much good. He'll find the arrow and figure me out in seconds, but it will buy me a head start, just enough for me to make it to where he'll never reach me. My cliff.

I dash through the stalks, shoulders shifting to dodge the leaves, so Father doesn't spot me too soon. Given how often my older sister, Niah, and I hid here during our seek-and-find games, I could do this blindfolded. But Father will uproot the whole plantation if that's what it takes to find me, so there's no sticking around. The cliff is the only safe place.

And there I plan to stay—up high, with my rope coiled out of Father's reach. It won't be much of a place to sleep, and the netherbeasts might come sniffing for me at night. But at least I'll be somewhere close to Niah. Stars know when I'll see her again if Father takes me to Grandfather's to—

My face slams into something hard and unexpected. I stumble

back, eyes fluttering to see what—or who—it is and find the unamused frown of our Head Bronze Guard, Hena. She grabs my arm before I can sprint the other way. My skin stings at her touch. These same hands arrested my mother and took her to Queen Solalé.

I should have guessed she'd capture me next.

"Got him, Alin," Hena calls into the cornfield.

A moment later, my father's sun-gold eyes are glaring at me, and all the heat of summer seems to burst against my skin.

"Let me go, Hena!" My voice is a parched sound. "He's gonna send me away!"

"Yeah, to Fenfyre, kid," she says, shoving me toward my father. "Take this as a blessing."

What do you know of blessings? I want to ask, but that's one of the few subjects that might reintroduce me to my father's backhand. Instead, I stuff it, like most things I'd like to say around here.

Father grabs me and twists me toward the town. "Makin' this harder than it has to be," he says. "Like everything else."

"This isn't fair," I protest, but I don't dare wriggle from his hold. "How can you send me away after what happened to Mother?"

"It's been nine months."

"Well, maybe I need nine years."

Father drags me onto the foot-worn path into town, putting the argument to rest with his silence. A strategy I could learn myself. One of the few things I could learn from him, anyway.

The quiet forces my attention toward the town. A sad sight, really. Crooked signs that screech for oil. Windows so caked in dust you can hardly see through them. Awnings that slant from the monsoon's beatings and busted signposts from netherbeast attacks. I try to picture it differently. Terragliders zipping down brick-laid streets and buildings that don't look like they're about to blow over. Towering walls lined with elite Bronze Guards protecting the city from netherbeasts. That's how Fenfyre is, Father says. But I don't care how nice it is. It's still the City of Bronze Guards—the same Bronze Guards who hanged my mother because of her faith in the Illuminant.

And Father expects me to make weapons in Grandfather's smithy for them. I'd rather stick weapons through them instead.

We pass the market and head down a short slope to our cobbled-together neighborhood. The path looked nicer a few months ago, when spring flowers still decorated the prickly landscape, but they're all dead now. Dead—much like how I feel realizing I won't see this place again until I'm old enough to come back alone. Father already warned me that Grandfather won't cover any travel expenses for me to visit, and Father himself can't visit except for this one time to drop me off.

How bad will Grandfather really be?

Mother sure made it clear she'd rather see me destitute in Jarden than living in Grandfather's lofty mansion, subjected to his hateful words and violent outbursts. And his esteem from Queen Solalé scares me even more. What kind of person does a queen from the netherworld favor? Those who are as wicked and ruthless as she is?

If only I lived in the days before Queen Solalé's reign—the days of the Illuminarchs. None of this would be happening then.

When we reach our doorstep, Father jerks me to a stop and faces me. "Now, listen here," he says, giving my shoulders a quick jolt. "Look at me."

I *am* looking at him, but he must have noticed I'm not looking to listen—I'm looking to see if he'll cry. Just one tear. That's all it would take to show me this at least hurts him a little.

His eyes are as dry and callous as the dirt on which we stand.

"Listening," I mumble, so he'll speak.

"You want to help this family? This is how you do it," he says, like he's delivering a battle plan to a soldier. "You listen to your grandfather and work hard. When you're ready, he'll hand you the smithy. Then you'll have all the money we need to get out of this beast-pit. To get us all safe."

My ears tingle at the thought of quiet nights for the rest of our lives—nights without the moans of nearby monsters, wondering if they'll come close enough for me to see. I've only glimpsed the silver-scaled tail of one netherbeast, just before Mother shoved us into her wardrobe as if a couple of wood doors would keep the beast from sniffing us out.

"You know it's just a matter of time," Father goes on, "before Jarden is invaded like Dunas. You're our only chance out of here."

His words stir up memories of our neighbors' stories—refugees from Dunas. The town, a hundred miles northeast of here, was once just as pathetic as ours. But their steward refused to demand his people attend the monthly honoring of Queen Solalé, so she revoked the Bronze Guards from their town and left them defenseless against the netherbeasts. Our neighbors are some of the only survivors.

"How long will it be before I can take over the smithy?" I ask.

Father's face loosens. "Don't know. About four or five years. Enough time for you to learn the works."

My lips twitch. *Sounds like forever.*

"Tell me you can do this, son."

The plea in his tone tenses my muscles. After all these years of talking to me like I'm a waste of space, suddenly, I'm my family's best shot at a secure life?

I shuffle my feet, considering it for a while.

"I'll do it." I submit like the good dog I am. "For Niah."

"Thatta boy." He smiles, patting my shoulder. "Now hurry up and get your things."

I'm still tempted to bolt for the desert again, but I go inside to do as he says. Our house is so small it takes about as many steps as I have years—twelve—to reach the bedroom door.

Inside, Niah sits on the edge of the bed with her dark curls hanging over her face like partially parted curtains. When I step in, she looks up and gives me a worn look.

"I don't see why you're running," she says. "Fenfyre is a beautiful city. You should be grateful you get to leave here before the rest of us."

I frown, and she stands with a long sigh.

"I'll miss you, pup." She rustles my hair like I'm five again, reminding me she's only two years shy of adulthood. "But it's going to be worth it. I'm sure Father only had a hard time there because he gave Grandfather grief. But you're not like that. You know how to listen. He'll be good to you. I'm sure of it."

I stare at the covered window, wondering how far I could get if I slipped out.

"Hey, at least you'll be able to fight netherbeasts for yourself someday," Niah says as she stuffs clothes into my bag for me. "That'll make you feel safer, won't it? You won't have to be afraid to go anywhere."

"What do you mean?" I ask, suddenly feeling like winter came too soon.

Her brow creases, but she releases a soft chuckle. "Well, they have to mark you, like Father. They do that to all Bronze Guard smiths, so you can test the magic weapons. I think they'll train you, even, since you'll be considered a reserve guard."

The bronze crescent will soon be tattooed on *my* skin? I rub my wrist in the same place Father's mark is. "But Mother said the mark is what makes Father act mean."

Niah slows, wringing a shirt in her hands. "Mother's faith is what upset Father, and the danger it put us in. The mark barely has any magic in it. It's not going to hurt you."

My vision blurs as she returns to packing. *Not going to hurt me?* How could she say that with how heartless Father is because of it? So heartless that he'd cast me off to Grandfather without remorse?

Niah's sniffle clears my eyes in time to spot a tear trickling across her tan cheek. Her tears are a strange type of magic. A summons for me to be her brave brother—her shield and armor against a wicked and terrifying world. To pay whatever price to keep her from crying again.

And now I know she's more scared for me than she's letting on.

I stand taller, forcing the fear to hide behind my feigned confidence. "It'll only make me mean if I let it. Nothing's going to change me, Niah."

Niah wipes the tear and presses on a smile. "That's better, pup."

I try to smile back.

Father's footsteps pass the door, reminding me I'm supposed to be hurrying. I dig a book my mother gave me from the back of my wardrobe—*The Book of Illuminance.* Mother used to read it to me when Father was away so I would know the truth about our kingdom's history and who our God really is—despite Queen Solalé expecting us to worship her like one.

Niah backs when she sees the book, as if me holding it would summon the netherbeasts here to kill us. She never cared to listen to Mother's readings, and it would take both hands to count the number of times Niah asked Mother to get rid of this.

Well, it's going now.

I wrap the book inside a shirt and bury it beneath the clothes Niah packed. If Grandfather finds it, I'll meet the rope that took my mother's life, but stars know I'm not leaving without it.

The buckles jangle as I pull the flap over and strap the bag shut, then I turn to Niah, a knot twisting in my stomach. Will we even be able to write? Or will Grandfather forbid that, too?

"Are you going to be okay?" I ask.

She remains silent, but my question pulls another tear from her eyes. It's the opposite of what I want. I want her to smile. I want her to laugh. I want things to go back to the way they were nine months ago, when the worst things happening to us were our parents keeping us up with their fighting and Father's drunken insults. And who'd have thought I'd ever miss that? But this is worse. A thousand times. A million.

But Father's right. There are also the netherbeasts to worry about. If I don't do this, there may come a day when leaving Jarden may not be a choice anymore. If we're even still alive to run.

"Let's go, Ezro," Father says, with a slap to the doorframe. "I'll be back, Niah."

I abandon my bag on the bed and rush to Niah, wrapping her in another hug, tight, like if I squeezed hard enough, we might become inseparable. I do my best to smile when I finally let go. "I'm coming back for you soon. I promise."

She nods, but she's crying even more now, and all I can do is stare at those tears. Streaking her face. Dripping off her chin. Summons after summons to be brave.

And yet, it's so hard.

I pull her back for one last embrace. "Nothing's going to change me, Niah," I swear again. "Nothing."

2

VAERYN

Six years later…

With a dust scarf wrapped over my mouth and a hood cloaking my pale hair from the morning light, I approach the gate of the last place in the kingdom I should be going. *Fenfyre. The City of Bronze Guards.*

A sweat builds on my palms as I cross into the shadow of the city's towering walls. The guards flanking the closed gate study me, and my heart palpitates. If they recognize my resemblance to my great-grandmother, the last Illuminarch, my quest will be over right here. And death would be a mercy compared to what that nether-witch queen would surely do to me once they turned me in.

But this is the last city I'll encounter before my journey leads into the wilderness, and thanks to a trio of thieves, I need to recoup my supplies first. They ambushed me a few miles back, making off with my hunting arrows, medicine sack, and a shred of my cloak before I could fight them off.

Desperation makes us into the worst version of ourselves. I'm no differ-

ent.

"Where are you coming from, lass?" the taller guard says, inspecting my dusty figure.

"If I could remember after the journey I've had, I'd surely say," I answer, briefly lowering my scarf to smile at him. "I'm a huntress from the north, but I had a rather unfortunate run-in with some bandits. Luckily, a Bronze Guard rescued me." *Lies,* but the kind that earn trust around here. "He pointed me toward this city."

The man turns and opens the gate.

Forgive me, Illuminant, I think toward the skies. Lying is the last way I should use my tongue, but I'd be dead if not for it. Once again…*desperation.* I hope to be free of it one day.

I step into the city. The metallic reek of nethermagic practically colors the air red, sickening me as I walk into its crowded streets. A terraglider hums past me, tossing my clothes in its wind. Sunrays glint on its polished white body as the hover vehicle weaves through the foot traffic ahead. A sharp female voice hollers at pedestrians to move, and people scatter. I follow her trajectory to a building towering like a castle over the town—the Bronze Guard Academy, no doubt, by the crescent flags jittering in the breeze. Inside its walls, young girls and boys are being indoctrinated to believe the queen's lies at this very moment.

The rider tweaks the handlebars, leaning her body to the left. The terraglider abruptly turns away from the academy toward another sector of the marketplace, within which, I spot a building puffing a cloud of smoke into the brilliant sky. *The smithy.*

Precisely what I was looking for.

I rush down the road, brutally aware of how my ragged appearance grabs everyone's attention. Mothers shuffle children away. Men scoff. But a firm glance from me scares their eyes back to where they belong—elsewhere—lest they look too long and notice I'm the spitting image of the kingdom's last rightful ruler.

My tatty boots march to the smithy door. A bell announces my entrance to the gray-haired master smith, interrupting what seems to be a lesson with his young apprentice. The smith sets his hammer beside the anvil. His crow-like eyes scan me from head to foot.

"I would like to purchase arrows," I say.

"You realize what kinda shop you're in, don't you?" The smith's voice grates like a grindstone.

Of course.

I glance at the weapon in his hand and the ones hanging on the wall behind him, all glistening in the light of flameless sconces. Only then do I notice crescent moons branded on all the weapons here, same as the ones tattooed on every Bronze Guard. Exclusive weapons, not to be handed to someone as *simple* as me. I should have guessed.

"This shop is for Bronze Guards only," the smith adds, as if I'm too dense to conclude it myself. His young apprentice leans against the back counter, pinching a laugh behind his smarmy sneer.

My face threatens to flush, but I broaden my stance. "Is there *another* shop I may give my money to?"

"You're in the City of Bronze Guards, *Northerner.*"

The smith says "Northerner" with enough spite to sting the fair skin he's gathered my heritage from. A temptation to leave to spare myself from paying this wretched man almost turns my heel, but I resist. Wretched or not, I need arrows to hunt along my journey. "No" is an unacceptable answer.

"I am well aware that I cannot use your arrows to their full potential," I say, softening my tone. "But I would like to purchase them, no less."

He steps closer. The heaviness he walks with could shift the world down an inch. "How much you willing to pay?"

I swallow. I hardly have anything left, and if I spend too much now, I'll have nothing for the way back.

There won't be a way back, I assure myself. *Not like the way I came.*

"I can offer twenty goldlets for a sheaf."

The master smith stares and stares and then laughs—a wicked sound, soon joined by his apprentice. I keep my face even, patiently waiting for him to lose humor and get back to business.

"That ain't nearly enough for these. Go somewhere else, woman."

No! I want to yell. *You can't send me away. I need these! How will I hunt without them?*

"But sir—"

He turns to his apprentice, his back like a door slammed in my face. "Better get to the academy, Brooks. Don't want Sterling to see you showing up late."

The apprentice nods to his mentor, then meets my gaze as he hangs his apron on a wall hook. His nasty grin grows as he crosses me, a sour remark surely tingling on his tongue. When he brushes a curl from his eye, I spy the bronze crescent on his wrist and almost feel sorry for him. Was the boy always like this? Or has the nether-magic in that mark squeezed all that was good from him?

The door shuts behind him, and the smith looks over his wide shoulder. "What are you still standing there for, woman? Get outta here. Twenty goldlets ain't gonna cut it for a sheaf of *branded* arrows."

"Then sell me a half sheaf," I say.

"Not wasting my arrows on somebody who can't use them."

My hand reaches to dig my last resort from underneath my shirt—a pendant only a Bronze Guard's wife would bear. But a voice from the side stills my hand.

"Then sell her these."

I turn to the far side of the shop. Another young man with black hair spilling just over the tip of his bruised ear holds the smith's gaze. A breath shudders into my lungs. How did I miss him before? He must've kept utterly silent there in the corner, watching this horrible conversation unfold. The blush I fought a moment prior now stains my cheeks.

The young man—another apprentice—strides toward a chest of drawers and rolls one open. Enough arrows to fill twenty quivers rattle inside.

"These are *common*." He shoots a look at the smith that could split bone. "Haven't etched them yet. Twenty goldlets will do."

The smith snorts, swatting toward him like he's a fly. Then he turns for the back door. The apprentice watches him leave with eyes like burning firewood, as warm as they are severe, but they soften as he turns to me and smiles.

I stall as if trapped in time, staring at his kind expression and the striking contrast of his ebony hair against his golden tan skin. Perhaps it's the bias of him interjecting to help me, but in these last four weeks I've spent in the south, I've yet to find such a comfortable gaze to rest in.

His smile wavers, and a flick of his gaze toward the back door reminds me we're running on his smith's patience, not an infinity. I step over, peering into the drawer beside him. The arrows inside are all identical, as if a man hadn't made them but a machine. He hands one to me, and I run a finger over the shaft, smooth as glass. The feathers are trimmed not a thread too long, and the black steel arrowhead is sharp enough to prick my finger.

Graces, these are nicer than the ones out on display.

"Just one sheaf?" the young man asks, waving a linen cloth to collect them inside.

"All I can afford," I admit.

He looks at the door again. "Do you need more?"

What is he doing? Trying to trick me into spending more than I plan to?

Or is this kindness?

"Yes," he answers for me, smirking like the other apprentice had, yet it doesn't feel malicious on him. "That quiver can hold more."

"Doesn't matter if I can't afford it."

"Doesn't matter if they're free," he says, counting off another dozen before he wraps them in the linen.

"But—"

The squint of his eyes stops me. "I made them. I'll decide what they're worth, not him. This way. Before he comes back."

I follow him to a standing desk where he lays the bundle. He grabs a record book and pen from the single drawer. As he flips to the current page, I notice a scar across his right cheekbone and, if I'm not mistaken, another bruise fading over his brow. The sight stings my heart after his kindness, and I lower my gaze down his labor-sculpted arm to the pen in his hand. In writing as pristine as his arrows, he etches "thirty-six arrows sold to," then looks up. "What name am I putting down?"

"Vaeryn Wilder."

My alias numbs my tongue with grief. *Vaeryn,* I am. But *Wilder,* I may have become, had my dearest friend, Verik, not died aiding me on this foolish quest of mine. Truly, I stand no chance without him. I need another Bronze Guard—someone who can fight the nether-beasts that my weapons cannot touch.

My brows furrow, gaze pinning on the bronze crescent on the apprentice's wrist. *What about this man? He seems... untainted.* No telling how long he'll stay this way. He must have gotten the mark recently, otherwise he'd be as revolting as the other two. But *perhaps* he'll remain decent long enough to protect me through the Creator's Canyon—

The tap of his pen draws my attention to his assigned price. *Ten goldlets.* I flinch, immediately shaking my head to refuse. I offered twenty goldlets for a sheaf. He can't sell me a sheaf and a half for ten! Won't the smith know?

My gaze returns to the healing bruises. What would he do to him?

Why is he doing this?

I hear a cough behind the door, and my hand dives into my coin purse, digging out the amount he's written. I pass it to him, guilt stinging like a sunburn.

He drops the slim coins through a slit in his safe. The machine beeps to count each one before it clinks to the bottom. Then he raises the bundle toward me, but my hands hang at my sides. He seems so benevolent. So unaffected by that mark.

Would he do it? Would he be willing to aid me through the Creator's Canyon? Surely, he has some training to face the monsters therein. All Bronze Guard smiths dual as reserve soldiers.

This could be the grace of the Illuminant.

Even if all I asked was for him to take care of that necromancer who's been trailing me for three nights—

The door swings open, and the apprentice shoves the bundle into my arms. A fleeting look of panic crosses his face before he covers it with a smile. "Take care," he says.

My bones weigh in regret, but it's too late. I can't say anything with the master smith glaring us down, cracking his knuckles like a threat that I've overstayed my welcome.

Or he knows what his apprentice has just done, and those fists are for him.

"Get going, lass," the smith says, "before everyone thinks we sell to commoners."

My gaze doesn't break from the apprentice's face, but even he's urging me now with a glance toward the door. I squash my hopes, recognizing them as selfishness, and fill my eyes with the gratitude I can't speak before I exit the shop.

3
EZRO

"Ten goldlets?" Grandfather's palm slaps the record book so hard that the display swords on the walls sing.

My body petrifies. What have I just done?

I blink, and suddenly, the book is hurtling at me. I shift to the side, pages fluttering next to my ear as it passes by. It hits the ground with a thump and a skid. Grandfather's heavy boots stamp toward me. Instinct screams for me to run or take up arms. Its voice grows louder the closer he gets. But obligation welds my feet to the ground, like always.

"What did I tell you last time, boy?" Grandfather's ale-stained breath puffs into my face.

His fists ball, and my molars sink into my cheeks.

"What did I tell you?"

I remember it...now, at least. The last time he mistreated a needy traveler, I sold my work for half-price. Grandfather let me, but as soon as the man left, he marched over, spitting in my face as he said—

"Try that again, and you're done," I repeat back to him, stomach

16

knotting. "But—"

He inhales the forge fumes, nostrils flaring, and I silence. His glower bores into me. Rage flickers in his eyes like a thunderhead, considering whether to strike. But he needs me, doesn't he? I'm the one keeping these walls full. Or have I just fooled myself into thinking I'm indispensable?

He has Brooks now.

"I'll pay the difference," I say, fingers trembling. "Just take it out of my allowance."

This stirs a hateful smirk across his face. "Ain't about the money, boy. 'Bout you stepping over me. You think you know better? You think you should already run this place?"

I search for the right answer, but there isn't one besides a lie. Father said Grandfather would hand me the smithy when I was ready, and I've been ready for two years. Yet, Grandfather is still standing over me, the same as he had when Father first abandoned me here.

"What's the matter with you?" Grandfather fills the quiet with another shout in my face. "Too dense to take an order? Or too stubborn?"

"I'm sorry."

He snorts. "Tell that to your sister."

His words hit me like the drizzle of rain before a downpour of realization weakens my arms. He really means it. He's firing me.

"Please, Grandfather—" Panic raises my tone. "I won't do it again. I promise."

"Said that last time."

"But I mean it." My fists ball as I step nearer to him. "I swear. Take what's owed from my allowance. Take all of it, everything I've cost you. I won't defy you again. Please."

He huffs, his long pause holding me in suspension. Just give me one more chance. One more. I can't fail Niah—

"Tell you what," Grandfather says with a sneer. "You go out there and get that Northerner to give back every arrow she can't afford, and I'll overlook it. Just this last time."

My chest tightens. Mercy isn't a language my grandfather knows. So, what's this? Desperation?

No. He wants to humiliate me. Send me out there like a dog with his tail between his legs so I can tell this girl I disserved my master, and now she needs to pay for it.

But how could I do that to her? To anyone? Who gives, just to snatch it right back?

"Better hurry before she's gone," Grandfather says, leaning close so I see every thread in his dark irises. "Or you'll be too."

I hate everything about this, but I yank my work apron off. Metal dust showers as I toss it onto the wall hook next to Brooks'. Grandfather gives me a twisted smile, ever the captain of my sails. He knows just what to say and when to keep me under his control. And I'm helpless against it unless I want to disgrace our family like Father and leave my sister in Jarden where she's vulnerable to the netherbeasts.

The sun glares overhead as I step outside. I scour the bustling market for Vaeryn's gray cloak, and after several sweeps of my gaze, it seems she's already left—taking my chance of redemption with her. But then the bakery door opens, and out she steps. She stuffs a small loaf of bread into her bag, then squints at the dangling shop signs. Her hood throws a mask of shadow across her eyeline and a scarf covers her mouth, but everywhere the light touches, her skin glows like the moon. It's a sight my eyes aren't used to, here where everyone's skin is as tan as the desert.

Why is she out here, anyway?

I crush my curiosity inside my fists. Doesn't matter. Just get the arrows.

I step into the street, weaving through people like the cornstalks back home. When I reach the bakery steps, her attention remains in the distance. I pry my mouth open and deliver a timid, "Hey."

Her shoulders jolt, but the moment she sees me, she lowers her scarf, and a gentle smile lifts her flushed cheeks.

"Have you come to collect the rest of what I owe you?" she asks.

The words I forgot to prepare along the way fail to form.

Grandfather knew I couldn't do it, I realize. That's why he set me up to this. To prove my weakness.

The thought stirs enough spite to pierce my senses. If helping people is weakness, I don't want to know what strength is.

"No," I say, but I immediately want to kick myself. "Just on an errand." Or something like that. "Then I saw you looking like you needed to be pointed in the right direction."

A warm gust tugs her hood back, unveiling a crown of frazzled ivory braids and a shining sunburn across her forehead. She quickly pulls it back in place. "The only right direction for me is toward the gate." Her northern accent decorates every word. "But that, I can plainly see."

"Alright, what's the wrong direction I can point you in since you're obviously looking for something?"

Her smile rises. "You're clever for a smith."

"Can't all have ingots for brains."

"I guess not." Her gaze lingers on mine but fades as though a sea of thought suddenly pulled her under. I soak in a chance to look at her—a rare thing for me, to really look at someone's face. See their eyes. Talk to them…without an authority figure tapping their foot nearby. And she's fascinating—either for the lack of time I've spent in front of someone new or simply because she is.

She's like a flower that just endured a violent storm. Beautiful and frayed at once. Delicate, yet hardy enough to stand up straight. But there's something more about her, I realize. She looks familiar, but I can't seem to place why.

"Are you visiting someone here?" I ask.

"No. Just passing through." She looks across the market again. "Actually, there is something you may be able to help me find. There must be an apothecary around here?"

"It's that way," I say, pointing down the main road. "Make a left at the fountain. It's the one with the"—my voice fades as I remember what I'm supposed to be doing—"yellow awning."

She nods, lips twitching like there's something else she wants to say. She glances at my marked wrist but meets my gaze again with renewed focus, as if deeming whatever else was on her mind unimportant.

"Thank you," she says. "And for the arrows. Kindness is a rare thing. I couldn't tell you the last time I saw it before today."

She steps away, and the word "Wait!" lurches from my mouth like a grappling hook. She turns around, knitting her brows.

My lips part to tell her what Grandfather sent me to do, and what it will cost me if she doesn't comply. But her last words echo in my ears, and all my intentions wither like grass at summer's peak.

"Yes?" she asks.

I swallow. "Maybe I should show you to it. Not everyone in Fenfyre is nice to strangers."

Her dirt-crusted fingertips fidget with the hem of her frayed cloak. "I'd hate to keep you from your errand. I've probably gotten you into enough trouble with that smith as is."

If only she knew how deep of trouble I'm in. That Niah's in.

A nervous twitch in my lip threatens my smile, but the tingling in my hands only worsens at the thought of her walking away. More time. That's what I need. Then maybe I can muster the courage to explain to her what's going on, and she'll hand back a few of those arrows.

"Really, it's not far. I don't mind," I say.

Her attention flicks to my bronze crescent again. "I suppose it wouldn't hurt to have a guide."

I glance the way I came, making sure Grandfather hasn't come to watch, but his shadow doesn't stain the ground.

"Follow me," I say, and start toward the apothecary.

Vaeryn's presence blares in the corner of my eye, and even with the two-foot gap between us, I feel like our shoulders are pressed together. When was the last time I walked around town with someone?

Since Jarden?

I lead her to a less crowded path—a mesquite-lined back way I often take to avoid the bustle. She looks at the signs and back to where I'd previously pointed. "Does this road also lead to the apothecary?"

"No, taking you for a tour," I tease, but my words lack the levity I'd planned for. Sweat builds on my palms. "It's a back way. Takes a little longer, but it's a nicer walk."

She watches her steps, her worn boots are a sad contrast to the pristine, brick-laid road. "Have you been working at the smithy awhile?"

Her curiosity almost makes me trip. No one's asked me about myself in so long, I can't even remember what the last question was or who asked it. Maybe Brooks? Before the mark got to him?

I fight a scowl. He and I were almost friends. Until Grandfather took to him like he was the grandson.

"I've been there six years."

"When are apprentices marked, if I may ask?"

I feel my steps slowing. "When they start."

But she's the one who stops and faces me, biting her scarred lip. "You've had that for six years?"

I check our surroundings. Only a few passersby are around, and none seem to pay us any mind. "Yeah. Why?"

Her chin tilts down, hiding her eyes. "It's just…most people who have it are…"

"Mean?"

She looks up. "Yes."

We hold each other's gazes, silent questions swimming in the space between us. Questions neither of us ask. But looking at her, my mind trails back to her familiarity. Something about her green-blue eyes and soft yet defined features seem like someone I've seen. But where? I've met so few people from the north, and none that I can remember were young women.

She clears her throat, stirring me from my trance. "Do you enjoy working at the smithy?"

"I will when it's mine." My answer reminds me yet again that my future is riding on how this conversation ends. "I'm supposed to take over someday. Hopefully soon."

Her mouth remains parted a moment before she seals her lips with a smile and signals us on with a nod.

I lead her onward, feeling every step as if ten pounds of steel were strapped to each ankle. When we turn back into the market, the shop's yellow awning announces that my time to speak up has almost run out. My tongue numbs, the words balling up in my throat.

"That's it?" Vaeryn asks, pointing.

I nod, but a wordless note escapes my lips.

Her head slants, and she waits expectantly like she knows I've forgotten how to speak.

"Nice meeting you," I finally say.

Her face tints a deeper shade of pink. "Same to you."

With that, she rushes off. My temples throb as she disappears inside the shop door. I could chase after, but I won't. I'm too weak, just as Grandfather thought.

But Niah.

I can't go back to Grandfather empty-handed.

I stand, mind whirling like a dust devil, until an idea strikes me. A terrible idea, but I've got nothing better. I pivot toward our neighborhood and bolt.

My hunting quiver rattles as I pull it off the wall mount in my bedroom. I spill the arrows across my bed—the same one my father slept in as a child—and count off the amount I need. My pulse throbs in my fingertips as I bind them. They look identical to the ones I sold—unbranded, crafted by the same hands. Still, that doesn't stop my anxiety from screaming. What if Grandfather finds out I'm tricking him?

My conscience can't decide if doing this is wrong or not. Does lying count when it's to protect someone else?

Mother seemed to think so. Otherwise, the Bronze Guards would have dragged me away with her to be hanged for our belief in the Illuminant.

I cradle the bundle of arrows and march back into town, praying Grandfather hasn't left the smithy. I scan every face as I walk. The people respond with upturned chins and averted gazes as if to remind me I'm nothing here until I earn my grandfather's title of master smith. It doesn't matter how well I perform at the academy or the quality of my weapons. I'm still the filthy, discarded boy from Jarden.

And maybe that's why I can't resist helping travelers like Vaeryn. They see me.

I swing my route wide so that it appears that I've come from the east wing of the market just in case Grandfather spies me on my way. The sun blazes against my back, heat pulsating across my skin as I approach the smithy door. Just set them down. Say nothing. It'll be fine.

The shop bell digs as I walk in. Grandfather turns from his anvil with a smile meant for someone else, by the way it flips into a grimace at the sight of me. His gaze snaps to the arrows in my arm.

A partial grin shows half of his yellowed teeth. "So, you had it in you."

My heart pounds double-time with his steps as he approaches, but I stand like a soldier and hold the bundle toward him. He snatches it, sneering with the satisfaction of a thief who got away. His calloused fingertips count each arrow's point before he carries it to the chest of drawers. My shoulders slacken as the drawer rolls open, dirt grinding in its tracks. With a pluck to the rope, Grandfather releases the binding, and the arrows clatter inside with the others.

It worked. Everything is fine. Niah's future is—

"Get out," Grandfather says, jabbing his thumb toward the door.

My body turns hollow. "What?"

"I said get out." Grandfather faces me. All the humor has washed from his face and been traded for something as dark as the pits the netherbeasts crawl from.

I stare, frozen in place. Does he mean for the day? Forever?

"You said if I got the arrows back—"

Grandfather's shoulders twitch. "Guess I'm not a man of my word. Besides, what do I need you for? Got Brooks. He'll make a fine smith. Never pulls any stunts. Been wanting to get you out of that boy's way, anyhow."

But I'm your grandson, I almost say, but then I remember Father. If Grandfather would dismiss his only son, why not me too? How could I be so reckless?

The ground seems to shift, the entire foundation of my world crumbling underneath me. I try to swallow but can't, to move, but my limbs feel separated from my body. What have I done?

Grandfather strides to the sword at his workbench. The blade whooshes as he swivels for the forge, holding the sword inside the flames. My feet impulsively slide back. One of those flanked across my back as a kid was enough.

"Well, get going," he says as the steel turns red. "And don't let me see you in my house when I get home."

Six years of disciplining myself to bow beneath this man's will almost pulls me straight out the door. But I can't. I can't just walk out. Niah is counting on me—

"Last chance, boy. If I turn and see you there, sending you off won't be the worst thing that happens to you."

I eye the sword, now orange. What does he think he's going to do? Strike me with it like before?

An invisible rope tugs me toward the bows on the wall. It would be so easy to take control of this and make him pay for everything he's put me through. The beatings. Insults. Seclusion. Treating me more like a slave than a grandson.

One arrow. Straight to the back of his knee. That's all I need to cripple his threat.

But what good would that do? He'd just have me arrested.

"Grandfather, why are you doing this?" I ask, a feeble hope convincing me I can still argue my way out of this. "How could you waste six years of training me just to hand the shop to Brooks?"

He pulls the glowing sword from the flames, but his back remains against me. "Because I'm not handing my shop over to a traitor."

Air jolts into my lungs and stays there until it's stale. Traitor?

"I'm not stupid, boy. I know you don't attend the queen's ceremonies. You reject her ways. Despise the guard. Have to be dense not to figure out why, knowing what your mother was."

Rage bursts across my body like fire dropped into a wheat field, but my voice comes out feeble. "You—you turned her in."

"What would I care what she believes?" His head shakes, a long silence following before he glares over his shoulder. "Why don't you go ask Niah what happened?"

Niah?

The burning on my skin turns cold. "How would she know?"

Grandfather faces me, a sick sneer on his face like the weapon in his mouth is fiercer than the one blazing in his hand.

"It was her."

4

EZRO

My thoughts race faster than my feet on my way to Grandfather's house. Niah? Niah turned Mother in?

Grandfather's lying. He has to be. It was him. He's the only one with the gall to do something like that. He just lied to get me away before I lost my senses and put him on the floor.

And yet—

If he suspected me too, why didn't he turn *me* in already? That would have cleared the way for Brooks. Was he worried about his reputation? How he would look for housing one of the Illuminant's Faithful? That must be it. That makes more sense than Niah. Who would report their own mother, knowing she'd be hanged?

I enter Grandfather's house for the last time with a shudder in my bones. A monster lives here—worse than the netherbeasts in the wilderness. His breath is still lingering in the air. His fingerprints mark every doorknob that I have to touch before I can get out. Forever.

I race down a hall lined with mirrors—I'll never comprehend how Grandfather hasn't shattered them at the sight of himself. I consider doing it for him. To trash the entire place, even. Make it look as bad as my memories of it. But the only good that would do is infuriate him enough to send after me. And it's not like he can't guess where I'm going. Especially after what he said. I have to confront Niah, to confirm he's lying.

My steps thunder into my room, and I lunge for the wardrobe, tugging out the old bag I brought here six years ago. All the letters from Niah—or the few that made it into my hands instead of Grandfather's forge—cover the base like a blanket.

My stomach swims at the sight. *What if Grandfather's telling the truth?*

I gather the letters together, uncovering a book wrapped in a small shirt. *The Book of Illuminance*, the last gift my mother gave me. I've pulled it out only a handful of times. The risk of Grandfather catching me with it was too great to take, but now, seeing it reminds me how afraid Niah was of it—how desperately she wanted Mother to get rid of it, like it was cursed.

Did she view Mother the same?

I leave the book where it is, then set to packing. When my bag is filled, I buckle my detachable quiver to the side and tuck my bow into the holster. After a quick redress, I strap on my Bronze Guard armor—a graduation gift from the academy—and try not to look at myself in the mirror. The bronze adorned armor and elegant cloak looks worthy of a prince, but it's branded with another crescent. Queen Solalé's symbol. Now I look just like the people who kill the Faithful. But it's my only set of decent armor, and who knows when I might need it.

I snatch my quarterstaff off the wall and twist it apart into two batons. The slick metal halves hang in holsters, one on each hip. I glance around my room. *What am I forgetting?*

Money.

I rush down the hall into Grandfather's room. The stench of ale-stained sweat emanates from his unmade bed as I step inside. I find his safe inside his equally reeking wardrobe and rotate the dials, trying the obvious codes first. His birthdate. *No.* His runaway wife's.

Winner.

The lock snaps, revealing heaping sacks of gold packed so tightly that I can barely yank one loose. He is legally required to pay me, not just toss me a few coins as an allowance. I take as much as seems fair and weigh my backpack down with it. He might notice, but he won't be able to do anything about it. I'm entitled to this money. He'd only get himself in trouble.

I return to the foyer and bid the house goodbye with a last look at its lofty ceilings and perfect floorboards—a beautiful place to lose your soul. I lock the front door behind me and drop my house key through the mail slit. Grandfather will hear it slide across the floor when he comes home.

I wonder if any part of him will be sad that I'm gone.

Sorrow crawls into my throat and burrows there, making it hard to swallow. I didn't realize how much childish hope I still had that he could become a father to me, since my real one rejected me. But Grandfather was worse. In every way.

I rush to the side of the house where the one good thing I've gotten out of this place sits—my terraglider. The chains jangle as I release it from its tether and clunk to the hard-packed dirt. I straighten the terraglider and straddle my leg around the slender vehicle. Settling into the leather seat, I knock the kickstand with my heel and crank the handlebars toward the brick-laid road. I hone my focus on the bronze crescent on my wrist, and a gentle tingle ignites the idle power within the crescent. I'd rather not use it. The power belongs to Queen Solalé, but nothing else will get me across the desert.

The energy extends from the crescent and illuminates a moon on the glider's front display. A gentle whir emits from the vehicle—the vibration of nethermagic running through its sleek frame—and the glider lifts off the ground. An exhale hisses through my clenched teeth as I press the throttle and speed down the neighborhood lane.

5

EZRO

DUST AND ANGER STING MY EYES AS I WHIZ BY SUMMER SCORCHED
trees and faded cacti. Wind stampedes over the lonely expanse, blasting against my right side and rocking my terraglider. I lean to regain
balance and accelerate. A storm front is marching over the Jeserene
Mountains, its shadow creeping into the valley where Jarden sits.
Normally, the smell of dust and rain in the air would thrill me, but
today I find it ironic. A storm darkened Jarden the day I left, now
another brews at my return.

Somehow that feels like an omen.

I tilt the handlebars, and the glider curves around a lone butte.
My pulse pounds with every stretch, knowing what awaits on the
other side. But when the stony wall recedes, and I see it—the vague
formations of the place I once called home—my mind numbs. I'm
like a ghost, returning to the land of the living, when everyone expects me to stay gone.

My terraglider slows when I reach the dilapidated wood fence
that serves as the town wall. A Bronze Guard stirs from beside the
crooked gate as if awaking from a standing slumber. I recognize her

in the glow of her lantern. *The wench who arrested my mother.* Her gaze trails from my glider to my armor, then she squints at my face.

"It's me, Hena," I say.

Her brow wrinkles, a hint of embarrassment in her eyes as she shakes her head.

She doesn't remember.

"Ezro Valorian," I say. "Alin's son."

Her jaw falls, and I wait for her to say something about it being nice to see me or asking how I've been. Instead, she says, "Oh. Carry on," and the gate screeches open.

I delay, tempted to ask her who reported Mother, but she's not permitted to say. Besides, I want to hear it from Niah's lips.

That it wasn't her, I pray.

I urge my terraglider into town. Ale and smoke permeate the air as I pass the first building, the tavern where my mother once worked. A sloppy patchwork on the door suggests someone must have punched it through…*again.* Or no one bothered to repair it in the last six years.

I ride through the pathetic market, disoriented despite how much time I spent on these dirt streets. Everything seems smaller and closer together than I remember. Even the way the torches gleam in the sinking darkness feels off. They should be higher up—brighter, maybe. The only thing that seems right is the annoying way the signs squeak in the wind.

I squeeze the brake when I reach the dirt road to the neighborhood and stare down its dark path. It's still and empty besides the spindly grass flickering in the wind, but it might as well be on fire for the way my mind screams looking at it. My old house is down there. And under its roof, Niah is probably finishing up dinner or readying for bed. Father might even be there, too.

What will they do when they open the door and see my face? Look at me the same as Hena? Like they don't know who I am?

My fingers crush around the throttle, and my terraglider bursts down the slanted path. I whizz past the first two neighborhood lanes, then take a sharp left onto the third. The magic in my glider snarls like a mountain lion as I rev it, clearing the distance in a matter of seconds before I come to a harsh stop in front of my house. *Father's house.*

I stare across the weed-ridden yard at the blackened windows. *Is anyone even home?* I squint at the entryway, looking for Father's boots outside the door. *Nothing.* Only a cluster of shed bougainvillea flowers rustling in the wind. *Must be at the tavern.* My lungs release their pent-up air as I park my terraglider at the edge of the yard. I march forward and halt at the door, bronze cloak flapping in the wind as I try to calm my nerves. *It wasn't Niah. Grandfather lied.*

Yet my nails nearly pierce my palms inside my fists. I pound the door and wait. For several seconds, I hear nothing but the stale flower carcasses stirring in the gusts.

"Niah!" I holler, pounding the wood again. "It's me."

A far-off thunderhead groans, but I hear nothing inside.

"Niah!"

When still no response comes, I swing my bag around and fish my old key from its depths. It shakes in my hand as I sink its teeth into the keyhole, and I have to fight to get it to turn. *Stupid, old door.* The handle crackles as I twist it and jerk the uneven door from its tight frame.

As I step in, a mildewy stench poorly coated with vanilla sneaks into my nose—familiar, yet far more aggressive than I remember. But it draws up memories of Mother so vivid, I almost fool myself into thinking she'll step from the shadows and welcome me back.

But she can't. She's dead. *Because of Niah.*

Grandfather, I correct myself, but it doesn't stop my voice from shaking when I call Niah's name into the dim house again.

The floorboards complain as I walk through the common room, scanning the familiar layout. Flattened couch near the window. Wobbly tea table over a faded rug. Nothing has changed besides the piles of dirty clothes and used dishes littering every surface.

Does Niah even live here anymore?

The question barely crosses my mind when footsteps creak from the hall. My attention snaps to the washroom door as the handle twists with a loud, metallic snap.

The door opens, and Niah's slender figure slips out, wet hair drooping past her shoulders. She freezes, gawping at me like I'm a netherbeast.

"E-Ezro?" she asks, squinting at my shadowed face. "Is that you?"

I nod, and a deep quiet unfolds between us.

For six years, I've imagined coming back to her, us running into each other's embrace, and me telling her I did it—I've saved her from Jarden. But now Grandfather's accusation penetrates through me like an arrow stuck between my ribs, draining all the air from my lungs.

Niah studies me, wet hair dripping onto her cream-colored nightgown. I recognize it by the blue flower embroidered across the scalloped collar—one of Mother's. A pang stabs my side. *How could she wear that if she's the one who did it?*

She couldn't. She *didn't* do it.

"Ezro? What's wrong?" she asks.

My lips beg me not to ask the question, even as it burns me from the inside out. But I can't leave it unspoken. I *have* to ask. I need to know.

"Do you know who turned Mother in?"

Niah's gaping mouth shuts, face turning toward her shoulder. Her age-defined jaw dimples before she loosens it with a wavering smile. "I—I don't know. I always thought Hena just caught her."

I step toward her. "Grandfather told me someone turned her in."

She brushes her wet hair behind an ear, failing to meet my gaze even when I stand just a reach away. I'm nearly a head taller than her now, and twice as wide. Four years her inferior, which used to feel like a whole generation. Yet now here I stand, her equal. Something that should have crept over us so slowly we almost didn't notice.

"Did he say who?" she asks.

A fierce gust knocks the window shutters outside. I listen to its angry howl as it blows by, wishing the wind could carry all this away from me.

"He said it was you."

Niah's brows dip, a tight scowl boldening her chin. "*Me?*" She attempts to laugh, averting her gaze again. A flare of lightning through the window dots her hazel irises and glistens along her moist waterline. "He was probably trying to cover for himself. I bet he did it."

I let her words hang in the air. They are what I want to believe. I want to blame him—send every ounce of my anger in his direction so I can have my sister back. Yet something inside me, deeper than emotion, deeper than knowledge, can sense it by her reaction. Grandfather wasn't lying. Not this time. And wishing isn't going to change anything.

"Grandfather never wanted anything to do with us," I say. "What reason would he have to turn her in? And how would he even know?"

Niah scratches her forehead, hiding behind her hand. "I don't know. Maybe he just wanted to ruin Father's life a bit more? Or wanted the reward?"

"But how would he *know*?" I ask again, firmer.

She stills, staring at the floorboards with a breath shaking through her lips.

"He didn't," I say, a frown dimming my words. "It had to be someone closer. Someone who was afraid of her—of her faith."

Niah looks up, a fresh flame in her eyes confirming my deepest fear. Her shoulders pull back and suddenly, she resembles Father—fierce eyes and harsh angles on her face. "The netherbeast attacks were increasing because Mother's faith lured them here. The entire town was in danger because of *one* person. Father and I tried to get her to give it up, but did she? No. She didn't care what it might cost the town. How many lives were at stake—"

"It *was* you."

Her nostrils flare. "I *had* to."

The air feels like it's passing straight through my body, like I'm nothing but standing bones. "You turned her in," I whisper.

The words hang between us like smoke, and we both stand, choking on it in silence. Our gazes burn into each other—mine, pleading for a different reality; hers, turning colder by the second.

"*You* turned our mother in!" I repeat in a shout. "How could you betray her—?"

"I *saved* this town," Niah yells over me, but her voice lowers with her gaze. "I couldn't take the guilt—every time Hena and her guard barely warded off a beast, I knew it was just a matter of time. We're vulnerable enough out here. The last thing we needed was a beacon signaling for the beasts to come here."

"But she's..." My words wither on my tongue as another betrayal rears its hideous face. "You—you wanted me to go to Fenfyre, to Grandfather's, knowing he'd brand me. You just wanted to get rid of me, too."

"That was Father's idea." She crosses her arms. "And I'll have you know, I hated it. But the beasts didn't stop coming after Mother was taken. I knew she'd been feeding you that nonsense, so when Father mentioned sending you to Fenfyre, I thought maybe you'd be straightened out before you had to suffer the same fate."

The hall seems to teeter. "So that's what sending me was about? Trying to break my faith in the Illuminant?"

"It's *dangerous*," she hisses. Her quieted voice reminds me we need to keep it down. "You know what the queen says. Netherbeasts can smell people's faith, and until every single person who still follows the Illuminant is gone, the beasts will never stop coming into this world. People like *you* are the reason innocent people are dying, Ezro. When are you going to wake up and realize that if the Illuminant still cared for us, he'd have done something in the last hundred years?"

My chest pulses as I try to gain control of my voice before my own shouts get me arrested too. "You really believe what the queen says? With all the wickedness she's done?"

"She was a *Radiant*, a right hand to the Illuminant, and she sacrificed her position in the Elysium to come down here. She risked betraying the Illuminant for *our* sakes. She's given *everything* to keep this world safe." She snatches my wrist, squeezing her thumb into the bronze crescent. "Don't you think this costs her something? To give *you* power?" She lets go, but tilts her face toward mine, so close our noses almost touch. "If she is so wicked, why does she share her power with men? Why does she fight the netherbeasts? Why doesn't she just let the world be overrun?"

"Because she's from the netherworld, and she's found herself a place to rule." I stand taller, as if to remind my voice to stay strong and not crumble beneath my older sister's dominance. "That's all netherbeings care about. Territory. Power. She's turned herself into a goddess in the eyes of man, why wouldn't she do whatever it took to uphold that?"

Niah gives me the same adolescent eye roll as she used to. "You really believe that? That our queen—*who kills netherbeasts*—is one of them?"

"Beings of the netherworld know nothing of loyalty. What is it to her to kill her own kin to gain our worship? Our compliance?"

Niah huffs, turning to rest herself against the hallway wall. "I see what good sending you to Fenfyre did. So is that all you came back for? To drill me about what happened to Mother, or did you come back to say you finally have a place for us to go?"

A coldness slithers through my ribs. "Forget about Fenfyre. I'm done serving the queen's henchmen." *Even if I still had a choice.*

"*What?*" Niah's tone hits a higher note. "You can't just drop our plan! You swore to get us to Fenfyre—to safety. You can't—"

"When was the last netherbeast attack?"

Her lips seal, a grimace hardening all her features.

"*When?*"

She looks over my head as if my eyes might kill her to look at. "*Years* ago. But there's been beasts in the desert nearby—"

"How many years?"

Her glower returns to me with such hatred I barely recognize her. "Since you left. Which means I was right. Ever since you and Mother were gone, Jarden has been safer. It's just as the queen says. The Faithful are what's endangering this world."

I force a full breath in and out before I speak again. "Well, then I guess you don't need to go to Fenfyre after all. I just need to leave, and you'll be fine." I march down the hall, a sharp pang in my heart announcing every step farther I take from my sister. My sister, who would send me to be marked for corruption and abused after she betrayed our mother to her death.

"You can't just leave," Niah says to my back.

I stop, fingers stilled over the doorknob.

"You worked for Grandfather for six years already, and you're just going to throw that away? You could be months, if not *days*, from taking over that smithy, getting us out of here—"

"Grandfather fired me."

Her words die in a gasp.

I swing the door open, a gritty gust blasting into my face, but I only get one step out before I nearly crash into a man. I stumble back, heart falling to my feet when I register his darkened face. *Father*. And by the fury in his irises, he heard what I just said.

6

EZRO

"Fired?"

Father's hands slam against my breastplate, and I stumble two steps backward before regaining balance. I raise my leather-clad forearm in defense, but his knotted fist doesn't swing. Instead, he steps back, looking me up and down with widening eyes—eyes that seem to register that he can't push me around like he did when I was twelve.

"What did you do?" he barks.

I watch him like he's a lion crouched to kill, noticing every new line on his aged face.

"It doesn't matter what I did," I say. "He was looking for a way to fire me. Told me himself."

Father blocks the doorway with his wide frame. "Tell me what you did."

I glance at Niah, her hand curls in front of her horror-struck face. *Afraid for me?*

No. For herself.

My eyes narrow as it hits me. *Father doesn't know she turned*

37

Mother in. She's afraid I'll tell him.

I face Father again, jaw tight. I could turn this whole conversation off me right now, redirect his fury to Niah. *But what would he do to her?*

The bronze crescent sparks like a shock of electricity, and a wicked thought shoots through my head. *He'd give her what she deserves.*

My mouth opens, and I hear a muted whine catch in Niah's throat.

"I was selling backstock, to unmarked travelers in need," I say.

Niah sighs, and I see her eyes squeeze shut in my peripheral vision.

"They were weapons I made myself," I add. "I cut them a fair price for common weapons. Grandfather didn't like that."

Father sucks his teeth, turning his face from me in disgust. I take his pause to look at Niah again, hoping to see a "thank you" in her eyes, but instead she's glaring toward my boots.

"How could you be so stupid?" Father spits, and my throat constricts. "Selling commoners weapons out of the most reputable smithy in Paran'dan? What did you think was gonna happen, boy?"

"I offered to pay for it out of my allowance." I keep my tone steady. "The world is dangerous. People need their weapons, if only to defend themselves against bandits or wild animals."

"And what about your family, and what they need? That worth the cost?"

Heat spills across my skin. "You mean the people who'd send a child as a living sacrifice?"

Father's chest broadens, his bloodshot eyes narrowing. "I was trying to get this family safe from the netherbeasts."

"Well, I heard you succeeded." I glance at Niah. "There haven't been any beasts in Jarden since I left. Maybe you should get out of the way so I can leave before my presence lures them."

I step forward, but Father's hand hits the doorframe hard enough to shake the paintings on the walls. "Go back to the academy," he orders. "Tell them you don't want to only be a reserve."

Air stretches my tight chest. My trainer, Sterling, wanted me to join the Guards. He said I was better with my staff and bow than most of my peers. I'd always told him I belonged in the smithy—carrying on my family's business—but that's only because I couldn't tell him the whole of it. I didn't want to be one of the people responsible for arresting the Illuminant's Faithful. Killing them. People like me. Like Mother.

"If you want to help people, that's how you do it," Father adds, voice calmer than before. "You fight the netherbeasts. Keep towns safe. And work your way up the ranks so you can get your family behind a proper wall."

"I'm not joining the Bronze Guard." I hold my tone firm. "You know what I'd have to do. And I won't. I'm not trading my soul for security."

His mask of composure melts. "Then what are you going to do, boy?"

"What does it matter to you?" I ask, eyeing the flashing sky outside. "As long as I'm gone, you're safe—"

"You promised to get your sister to Fenfyre, that's what it matters."

"Well, I can't."

Father smacks the door frame again. "I just told you how you can!"

"And I told you I'm not doing that." My gut suddenly feels punched. "When is it ever going to matter to you what I want? Has it ever crossed your mind that I don't *want* to live in Fenfyre and serve Bronze Guards in any capacity? That I might have something else in mind for my future?"

Father scoffs, a perfect reflection of his own father. "Like what?"

"I—"

My words seem to fall off a cliff as I realize I'm not even sure what my "something else" is besides that it doesn't involve the Bronze Guard. All the things I've ever fantasized about are idealistic and impossible in this world. Living a peaceful life. Meeting some-one. Maybe having a family and teaching them the same truths my mother instilled into me. But there is no such thing as a peaceful life with the constant threat of netherbeasts. And what good would meeting someone and starting a family do when being around me—a Faithful—just makes them a target?

"Well?" Father urges, shaking his head. "You don't have any plans. Just being rebellious. *Selfish.*"

I suddenly feel every mark Grandfather put on me afresh—the bruises, the scars, the crescent. "Don't call me selfish when you're the one who sent me away for your own gain. You knew what Grand-father would do to me. You've been through it. How could you send me to the same place that broke you?"

"To promise you a secure future."

I raise my marked wrist. "A secure future? Or a cursed one?"

Father casts his gaze to the floor, his frame bowing in.

"It was never about my future. Or anyone's *safety*. It was about you wanting to go back to Fenfyre. To reclaim your former glory. Your clout. Otherwise, you'd have let me walk out of here a minute ago."

Father hangs his head, his overgrown gray hair blocking his eyes. I wait for his response, feeling Niah's stare on us both. Her wordless, cowardly stare.

Finally, Father looks up and mutters, "I thought you'd be the son my father always wanted."

The disappointment in his hard stare crushes any hope I had that I'd gotten through to him. I swallow a lump in my throat. "Well, apparently, I'm the son nobody wants."

I shove him aside and rush into the windy yard.

"Fine! You wanna abandon your family? Do it!" Father shouts after me.

I mount my terraglider, not bothering to pay him another glance. I don't want to see it—the hate in his eyes, Niah standing like a loyal shadow behind him.

"If I see your face again, I'm reporting you," Father adds as I ignite the engine. "Don't think I don't know."

My hands freeze over the grips. *He'll report me.* Just like Niah did to Mother. Does family mean nothing to them? To any of them? Have I been nothing more than a slave all these years?

I inhale, breathing in the blowing dust. My fingers are just curling to press the throttle when Niah's voice pierces through a roll of thunder. "Where will you even go?"

My lips fight to stay straight. "To find somebody who sees me."

7

VAERYN

RAIN. BEAUTIFUL, PERFECT, COLD RAIN.

It falls like a gift from the Illuminant himself. A gift worth enjoying from the comfort of the small covering I found in the Jeserene Mountains. I watch water jutting off the rocks overhead, splashing the already flooding ground. A mist wafts into my face and decorates my dark leather sleeves with little dewdrops. In their tiny spheres, I can almost see memories. Days spent under the trees in Brïsbrook with a fog planting kisses across my skin. Across Verik's. His face shining in the peeking sunlight. Blue eyes like rivers of life welled up from his very soul.

Rivers of life that my choices dried out.

The heaviness of grief pulls me. Unrelenting. Selfish. Clingy.

When will it ever relent? Or is this my punishment for leading my dearest friend to his death?

I settle deeper into the nook in the mountain. The scent of the rain follows me even as I escape its gentle mist. I gather the kindling I've collected and perch the little twigs together into a steeple. I strike a match and hold it to a dried leaf, then lay it blazing into the wood.

My hands cup around the solo flame, and I blow until my breath brings the fire to life.

I retrieve the loaf of bread I purchased in Fenfyre and finally let my exhausted body rest against my stony refuge. The bread is stale at the ends, but I hardly mind. The taste is sweet after the journey I've had. Though…not every part of my journey has been unfortunate of late. Not that I should consider my experience in Fenfyre fortunate.

My gaze lands on the dark burning wood of my humble campfire, transporting me to the eyes of a stranger. A stranger who may have been with me, had I asked for his aid. The acidity of regret coats my tongue. While he may not have the firsthand experience Verik had, even Bronze Guard smiths undergo combat training and serve as reserve soldiers in case the netherbeasts become too powerful. Any help from that apprentice would be better than nothing.

But he was far too kind to burden him with my mess. I'd rather die one step into the canyon alone than make it ten at the cost of another man's life.

With a sigh, I retrieve my journal so I can awkwardly juggle my pen and bread while I write about the last few days' events. I spend far more ink on this stranger than what feels appropriate, and in some way, it spoils the taste of the bread. Verik was the only man I ever wrote in length about before, and now some smith's apprentice is occupying what little space I have left in this journal. But what else have I to write about anymore? Haven't I said enough about bandit ambushes, attempted arrests by Bronze Guards, rapid flights from netherbeasts, and hopes against hope that I make it through the Creator's Canyon to find the Etherium?

I let myself indulge, writing every detail I can remember from our brief encounters. But no matter how many words I scribble down, it doesn't satisfy. It never does. The pages don't speak back. They don't react. They just hold my thoughts in front of me like a mirror reflecting my heart, exposing the sea-deep void within me. I shouldn't be here alone. I shouldn't be here *at all*. This was Father's task—*his* dream. To journey through the Creator's Canyon and find the portal to the sacred realm where Illuminarchs are anointed in the Light of the Luminors. It was Father who dreamed of claiming his rightful power and wielding it against that vile netherwitch, Solalé. Not me.

But Father waited too long, and an injury thwarted his plans before he could ever set out. And graces know my cowardly brother, Liander, wasn't man enough to go in our father's stead. He wasn't even man enough to accompany me.

So here I am, defenseless against the monsters ahead, yet too afraid to ask the one safe man I've encountered for help.

My hand is aching around my pen when a noise whitens my knuckles. *A yipe.* Then a series of them. Their breathy resonance holds me stiff. Three nights of hearing their otherworldly choir has trained my ears to know them. *The necromancer's coyotes*—spirits my weapons cannot touch.

My face squeezes, muting my frustrations. Just one night. Just *one*, that is all that I want. One night to sit by a fire and listen to the precious sound of rain. To eat until my stomach is truly full and fill my pages in peace.

But never. The necromancer would not be so kind, and if my blade could kill him, I'd do it twice.

In flustered motions, I repack my bag, stamp out my fire, and throw my hood over my head. The downpour muffles the yipes, but there's no question that they are coming closer, and if they find me in here, I'll be trapped. Which means I must spend another night running. And running. And running.

Graces, how I hate running.

I step out, rain pattering against my hood, and detect the direction of the coyotes. I turn myself the other way, leaving my lantern unlit. My eyes are so used to darkness that even with nothing but the flashes of lightning to guide me, I'm able to navigate the terrain with moderate ease.

I stay as close to the mountain as I'm able, moving quietly under the splattering rain. If I can just get far enough ahead to where the necromancer and his dogs can't detect me, perhaps they'll lose my trail. Though I doubt it.

Raphós, where are you?

I scan the dark skies, wishing to see luminescent wings swooping to my aid—the wings of Raphós, the spirit who once led my earliest ancestor on this same quest. He's come to my rescue before, but rarely. Too rarely to count on.

Still, what else have I but hope?

My feet can't have carried me more than a mile from my comfortable nook before I hear a howl. The dreadful noise pierces into the very marrow of my bones. *They're close.* Fear heightens my senses—about the only thing it's good for—and suddenly the world around me feels alive. The mountain is a guardian at my right, standing tall in his armor, holding back the winds. The rain murmurs across the earth as it rolls downward. A guide toward the most level ground. I follow it. The lightning flares like winks from the Illuminant, reassuring me he is here, ever looking after me. He will see me to the Etherium. He will send Raphós—not a moment too soon or too late.

I tell myself a sheaf's worth of times that I trust him. *I trust him. I trust him. I trust him.*

Though my feet may slip on this slick ground, my faith cannot— will not—be shaken. There's too little of it left to lose.

I use my breaths to mutter the prayer my father once taught me. "I will not perish, for the Light is in my blood." My boot skids in the mud, and I barely catch myself on a rock wall. "And where the Light goes, the darkness cannot follow. The Light is in my blood."

It comes out in a song as I repeat it. I sing it in harmony with the soprano howls of the coyotes, over and over, like the song itself would save me. But deep within, I know it won't do any more than my unmarked sword would against these dogs. The Light in my blood is what they are salivating for.

A scream suddenly shatters our duet. *My* scream. A noise that splits through the rain and reverberates up the mountains and into the black sky. There—right before me—the necromancer has emerged. The deer skull he's claimed for his face points straight for me, his weed-ridden, hollow eyes locked on my flesh. I step back, only to hear a canine snarl at my heels. The briefest glance behind shows the spectral pack. They've found me at last. Surrounded me. Back, to the coyotes. Face, to the beast himself.

Raphós! I scream inside my soul.

I draw my worthless sword. It will slip through him like a hot knife through butter, but stars be dimmed if I don't die holding my dignity in my hand. "Get away from me!" My voice is as callous as the canines'.

The necromancer slants his head, his branchlike horns scratching the rocky mountainside. The rain washes through his exposed bones, a soft trickle like a fountain—a noise not unlike what my blood will sound like as it drips onto these stones. But the necromancer himself is silent. No heartbeat. No breath. Only a soul holding together these gathered branches and bones. A soul mine will belong to if I die by his bidding.

The necromancer lifts his wooden staff, a ragged blade held in his other hand, and swipes. I duck. A second of blurred time passes, and I'm running again.

The coyotes yelp in frustration, and I hear a hiss from the necro-mancer. A netherical whisper—a command. The dogs excite, leaping into action. Their grunts and cries sound ravaged. A sound that clues me into what the necromancer must have said.

Feast.

I run fast and reckless. Skidding, fumbling, hitting my armored shoulders on branches and cacti, until suddenly my toe butts a rock. I fall, hands scraping the wet earth, and a dog jumps on my back. I roll, swiping at it, but my sword passes through it, despite how the spirit could weigh on me. Nonsensical. Just like everything from the netherworld. I roll again, hand finding a branch, and tug. I scramble upright, teeth gnashing after me. My feet burst forward, but my heart is ringing a bell of resignation.

I can't outrun them. Not in the rain. The beautiful, perfect, cold rain.

It will be what buries me.

8

EZRO

MY LEGS DANGLE OVER MY OLD PERCH, A LEDGE ON THE CLIFF SIDE A short ride from town. Beneath me is a darkness as hollow as my bones. *Niah turned Mother in. Just as Grandfather said.*

And Father would do the same to me.

After all I suffered for them.

I rustle my wind-wrangled hair. Mother used to say the surest sign of love was to lay one's life down for another. But where is the line drawn between sacrificial love and suicide?

Is it here? Realizing they have no respect for my life? Or is there no boundary between the two, and I'm to give until I have nothing left?

I stare into the blackness below as if the answer might emerge from it. Lightning flashes, exposing a landscape of tall saguaros and crooked bushes. Their shadows flicker and fade, then everything is darkness again. Instinct starts me counting the seconds before the thunder. I get to four before a rumble shakes from the clouds.

I sigh into a dusty gust. The storm is almost here. I should climb down before the lightning comes close, but I can't muster the strength to move my legs. *Let the lightning come. It's not like I matter to anyone.*

The dark thought jars me. Mother never liked when I said things like that out loud, but how could she defend against it now? What could she say to lighten this? There's nothing that could fix this. I've ruined everything, and even if I hadn't, my life before was a lie.

I pull my backpack closer and dig out *The Book of Illuminance*, as if touching its pages might summon Mother back to me. I unwrap the text, revealing its supple leather cover. Five entwined swirls emboss the center, once brilliant gold, now flaking and dull, but it still illuminates in the darkness. My frown sinks into my cheeks as I imagine Mother and I sitting together in the corner of my childhood room. She'd read it to me while Father was busy in his metalworking shop, on the rare occasions when she wasn't working, too.

I open it, and a soft glow emits from the pages. Mother said the Illuminant blessed the book in this way, so that even in the darkest places, the Faithful could still read the truth.

My finger traces Mother's note to me on the front page. *Never change.*

Almost as if she knew what was going to happen.

I fan the pages, having to fight the wind to hold them down. The first section is instructions on remaining upright as one of the Illuminant's Faithful. The next recounts the histories of the Illuminarchs, the Illuminant's anointed rulers. My mother read them to me when I was too young to remember them well, and I haven't bothered to read them again. It infuriates me to think about the way things were versus the way things are now. But I find myself thumbing past them slower, admiring the illustrations of each Illuminarch at the start of their biography. They and their divinely gifted counsel all bear markings on their skin—elegant scrolls in various designs. The marks of the Luminors.

Much different marks than what stains my skin.

I'm about to shut the book when the wind flutters the pages and lands on the introduction to our last Illuminarch, Athenias

Seraphine. My body freezes, eyes locked on Illuminarch Athenias' face. Pale skin. Ivory hair. A soft yet strong facial structure.

She looks almost identical to that traveler, Vaeryn.

I blink, shaking my head as if to clear whatever illusion I'm seeing. But the image looks exactly the same when I look again.

She couldn't be related to her, could she? A descendant?

What was she doing out here?

My gaze snaps to the flashing desert. Far beyond the Jeserene Mountains is the Creator's Canyon, in which the portal to the Etherium lies; a holy realm where the Light of the Luminors rests. This Light was granted to Paran'dan—the capital of the world—after Creation. It was the Illuminant's gift to mankind to supernaturally empower those he elects against the netherworld. But only someone from the Illuminarch's lineage can claim the power, and it's been a century since anyone from the bloodline has been detected.

But what if Vaeryn *is* of the lineage? What if *that's* where she's headed?

A chill layers over my skin, then slowly melts. I'm thinking nonsense. There's no way Queen Solalé or the netherbeasts would allow any trace of the Illuminarch's lineage to survive. It's a coincidence. A false hope. My emotions are just messing with me.

I tuck the book away.

A cold drop splats against my hand, then I notice the soft thumps in the desert below. Slow, dense raindrops. The kind that foretells a heavy rain is to come.

I really should get down.

But as I shift to move, a hollow call resounds over the wind and rain. My head turns each way. The howl seemed to come from everywhere. Behind. In front. Above and below.

A series of yipes follow—coyotes. But their ubiquitous sound prickles the hair on my nape.

I stand up, squinting into the obscure distance. Little white figures appear, gently glowing against the blackness. My muscles tense. In all my years at this cliff, never once did I see anything strange in the desert. But then again, Mother never allowed me out here at night when they emerge.

The figures race closer, their voices loudening every stretch they cross. Their canine forms come into focus—coyotes, all right. But not ones that are living.

Ghosts.

Another sound reaches my ears—the steady pound of shoes against the hard-packed dirt.

Is someone out there? Or am I just imagining it?

A massive lightning bolt fills the entire horizon over the Jeserene Mountains. In its fleeting, flickering light, I spot a cloaked figure bounding straight toward my cliff. The spectral dogs are but a reach behind.

I snatch my bow and nock an arrow in record time, but hesitate with it on the string. I can't see the runner, just the ghosts, and there's wind...

My finger draws the string anyway, and the crescent on my wrist kindles with a fire-like burn that singes my entire hand as the power channels into the arrow. A glow of orange activates the matching moon on the shaft, enabling—hopefully—my arrow to touch the ghost as though it was solid matter. I've never done it myself. Only tested to ensure the weapons in the smithy would ignite.

I trail my target and wait for the next flash of lightning so I can see the runner. Then I release the arrow, holding my breath as it pierces through the blackness.

The coyote nearest to the runner puffs into mist.

The yelping pack staggers to a stop, and the corner of my mouth flinches up. *Weren't expecting that, were you?*

Me neither.

I ready the next arrow and wait for the lightning, but when it flares, I see something else standing in the desert—a tall figure with antlers branching from his deer-skull head and a feathered staff clenched in his fist. A memory surfaces from the books in the Bronze Guard Academy of a netherbeing whose magic shames most any other.

A necromancer.

The lightning bolt dissipates, but I feel as if it left its electricity inside my veins. A *necromancer* is out there—a real one, not just an illustration in my study books—and it's chasing someone.

Why is that person out there, anyway?

There's no time to ponder it. The coyotes are racing again, and the wind is picking up, making my aim unsteady.

I need to get down there.

I toss my bag over the edge and downclimb by the decade-old rope from my childhood. It's still impressively sturdy, though I hear a few threads snapping on my way down. I drop halfway, landing with a loud thud, and trade weapons out. Arrows will prove nearly worthless against a creature made of wood and bone. But my quarterstaff—I twist the metal halves together and ignite the crescent—is a worthy weapon.

I race toward the spectral figures. The runner's form is clearer from the ground. Her high-pitched breaths reveal her as a woman, but before I see her face, she abruptly turns and runs away from me.

"No—" I say, but I forget to finish when I hear the necromancer whispering like wind hissing through cracks of stone. In an instant, all the dogs turn from their previous prey to me.

I sweep my weapon, knocking back the first coyote that gets close. It falls to its shoulder with a yipe that stills its companions again. I hold my staff out, the metal ringing in my hands. My eyes dart between each of the coyotes. The full pack—six of them—are here now, but they seem uncertain.

Where's their master? Has he gone after the woman?

I don't look for him. The coyotes are watching my gaze too closely. One distracted glance and they'll be on top of me. I prod the end of my staff toward them—*back, get back*—hoping they'll slink away. Instead, they circle me. *Smart things.* I can't watch them all. I rotate, constantly snapping my gaze from the ones on my front, to my sides, to behind. My staff turns with my eyes, waiting for one of them to break from formation and strike. But they keep circling me, slow and hungry.

One finally bursts after my heel from behind. I twist and pummel it in the head so fast that I don't register it until a pale cloud of dust is dissolving where it stood. Another leaps from the other side. I bash it. Straight under the jaw. Then all at once, the rest lunge toward me.

I spin and swing my staff in a dizzying flurry until the coyotes are shrinking back. *Cowards.* I almost laugh in relief, until I remember the necromancer and the woman. Where are they?

In the pause, I try to listen for her steps, but now rain is thudding the landscape like thousands of tapping fingers. It patters all over my arms—cold, invigorating drops.

I turn to finish the coyotes off, not trusting them to leave me alone, but as soon as I raise my staff, the pack turns and bounds into the distance.

Toward their master?

I race after, praying this doesn't mean the netherbeast has captured his victim—that I'm too late.

I fumble through the dark desert, probing ahead with my staff. *How is this woman seeing out here?*

I have so many questions. I hope she's alive to answer them by the time I catch up.

The specters stop ahead of me, and another flash from the sky brightens my view. I spot her, backed against another cliff—her pale face gaping in terror at the looming beast before her.

Wait—

Vaeryn?

I squint, noticing a lock of ivory hair beneath her falling hood. Then I see the rips in her cloak, and her newly stocked quiver.

It has to be.

My spirit enlivens, reminded of her striking resemblance to the last Illuminarch. If there's even a *chance* she is a descendant—

I charge forward, letting out a cry to alert the necromancer he'll have to deal with me first. His pointed muzzle turns, the crooked blade in his hand lowering from the strike he'd intended for Vaeryn.

She slips away, unnoticed, and I clench my staff tight, readying to face my first netherbeast. But the necromancer sees his victim is missing, and in the blink between flares of lightning, he and his pack dissolve into the darkness.

My feet slow, staff still raised like he might reappear a foot in front of me when I let down my guard. But several moments pass, and my shallow breaths deepen. I lower my weapon, rain dumping over me as I scan the obscurity for Vaeryn.

"He's gone," I holler.

No one answers but the thunder.

I start in the direction she ran, calling out every few steps. Each flash of lightning, I turn a full circuit, scanning as much of the desert as I can before the light goes out. But there's no trace of her anywhere.

"There's a town close by," I shout. "You're not safe out here."

Nothing.

Why would she run away? Doesn't she know the necromancer could come back?

But then the bronze of my cloak catches in my peripherals. *Because she thinks I'm a Bronze Guard.*

I swallow, body pulsing with adrenaline. A woman, nearly identical to the last Illuminarch, is out in the desert alone, being chased by a necromancer—of all beasts—and she ran from a Bronze Guard?

She did seem anxious to leave in the market.

My nails sink into my palms. The longer I consider it, the more likely my theory seems. What else would she be doing in the south? Why else would she sooner risk the necromancer's return than for a Bronze Guard to interrogate her?

I call out again, jogging a few more steps, but when she still doesn't answer, I retrieve my bag and run back for my terraglider. Descendant of the Illuminarch or not, she's in danger out there, and stars know, I need something to do tonight.

9

EZRO

I SOAR THROUGH THE DESERT LIKE MY MEMORIES ARE CHASING ME. My terraglider hums at an octave I've never heard; its speed is so fast I can barely dodge the saguaros. But it keeps me focused—distracted—as I scour the dim landscape for Vaeryn.

Moonlight rolls in as the clouds, exhausted of rain, peel from the sky. Its mild glow glosses the wet terrain but does little to illuminate the valley. I send more power into my terraglider's headlight, and its strength increases, cutting through the darkness like a beacon. But after a while of scoping the desert, I turn back for the area I first saw Vaeryn in case she left any form of a trail.

I slow my terraglider to a crawl as I approach my cliff. The glider lowers to the ground, unable to maintain levitation at this rate. I tighten my hold on the handles, having to fight to keep it straight over every little bump the wheels ride over. My headlight streaks the ground as I search for footprints, but the rain seems to have washed all evidence away.

"You don't have to hide," I holler, as if she might be near enough to hear me. "It's just me. The apprentice from Fenfyre."

Although now that I've said it, I wonder if I've made it even worse than her just assuming I'm a regular Bronze Guard. Last she saw me, I was standing next to Grandfather while he cracked his knuckles. Now, suddenly, I'm in the Jeserene Desert looking for her?

I scowl. There seem to be two types of women from my sparse interactions with them. Some who would find this charming, and others who would label me a predator. Something tells me Vaeryn falls under the latter category.

Either way, only silence answers me.

I look toward Jarden. A thought to abandon my search and go find someplace to spend the night flashes and fades like the lightning. My thumb presses the throttle, and I launch further into the desert.

I steer into a mountain's shadow and slow at the sight of a crusted footprint. After a long night searching, *finally* there's a sign of her.

I ease closer to check for others and spy the impression of a boot heel on the mountain slope. A muddy print stains a rock a few paces higher and, above it, I spot another. *Guess she went climbing.*

I pull my glider aside, knocking the kickstand down. Its loud, metallic clang echoes across the stony mounts, and I cringe. There goes what little stealth I had.

Dirt grates under my boots as I begin the ascent. The feeling is familiar, comforting. Father used to bring me to these mountains on hunting trips when his metalworking shop wasn't pulling in enough money. His degrading comments had laced the hours we spent out here, but I eventually learned to tune them out like the incessant buzzing of cicadas so I could enjoy the hike.

A rock loosens underfoot, pulling me back into focus. I lift off it gently, muscles tight, anticipating it to fall and *clunk, clunk, crash* down the slope. But it remains in place for now, and when I look up again, I realize I'm nearly to the top.

I scan for footprints again, but the mud she tracked must have worn off by the time she reached the solid quartz summit. My shoulders droop, eyes surveying the surrounding peaks and all the rocky hills in between. Miles of hiding places lay before me, days of searching, and for all I know, she's high-tailing it to Fenfyre or Rōsrun right under my nose.

It's pointless.

And I wish I knew why that irritates me so much; why I want so desperately to find her. Am I *that* aimless? *That* concerned about somebody I don't even know?

Or that foolish to hope there's a chance she really is a descendant of the Illuminarch, and she's trying to reach the canyon and save the kingdom?

I huff a laugh at myself. The more I think about it, the stupider it sounds. She's just a woman from the north, probably trying to reach one of the east towns, and somehow, she got herself lost out here. But even if that's all she is, she'll be in danger again as soon as the sun sets—provided she's still alive. I can't just leave her out here.

I train my eyes on the ground and press on, hiking until I stand at the summit. The Jeserene Desert stretches from one end of the horizon to the next, and far in it, the glint of Fenfyre pricks me like a thorn in the eye. I avert my gaze to Jarden, a pathetic splotch of civilization barely visible around the buttes between here and there. But even from this far, Niah and Father's words seem to echo across the landscape and skewer my heart.

Why'd you even come back here?

Selfish.

I thought you'd be the son my father always wanted.

I avert my gaze from Jarden, and the memories dissipate, leaving a cavity in my chest. *Vaeryn.* I was looking for Vaeryn. Someone who—if nothing else—showed at least a fraction of concern for my existence.

Is that why I'm so worried about her?

I creep around the summit, scanning every bush and boulder until I notice something pale flickering in the breeze. I cage my breath and lean closer. Fabric. *Gray* fabric.

Same as Vaeryn wore.

My mouth can't decide whether to smile or grimace. I found her. I *actually* found her.

Only…now what?

10

VAERYN

The footsteps stop. Close. I notice the hem of my cloak has spilled from my covering. I scowl but leave it. To pull it would give me away if this man—the Bronze Guard from last night, no doubt—hasn't already spotted it.

He clears his throat, and I grip my dagger, praying he won't make me use it. *Just walk on. Leave me be, and you go home unscathed.*

But then he takes another step, and his shadow creeps over the boulder. Armed, I see, by the outline of his bow and quiver. My bottom lip curls beneath my teeth and a silent inhale swells my lungs, fueling me for battle. Surely, he's been hunting for me all night, and determination like that can only mean one thing: he's noticed my resemblance to my great-grandmother and means to turn me in.

I fight an urge to peek around the boulder. *What's taking him so long to strike? Are there others? Has he not noticed me?*

I watch his shadow, expecting to see him beckoning someone or readying an arrow, but all that moves is his waving cloak and his head as he looks across the mountain. Searching. But for what? To be sure I'm alone? Checking for escape routes so he can prepare himself for pursuit?

My fingertips tingle against the cool grip of my sheathed dagger. I hear my every breath like they were howling winter winds, giving me away. They are the only sound in the entire desert besides the distant cooing of a quail—until the dirt crunches beneath his shoe again. His shadow shifts away. I almost smile, but then he turns, an arm reaching for the boulder—

My hand slips from my dagger, and I leap from my covering.

"Wait!" the Bronze Guard hollers as I sprint recklessly down the slope.

I could laugh. *What makes you think I'd listen?*

His swift footfalls chase after me, much faster than my own and more adept, like he was born right here in this mountain range. My feet skid and fumble. Rocks crumble beneath my feet. I hear his breath puffing closer, can nearly feel the warmth of his hand reaching to snag me by my hood.

I force my feet quicker, only to land on a rock that gives way. I slip to my back, skidding several yards before the slant eases enough to catch me in its stone-hard palm. Wincing, I gather back to my feet and bolt, ignoring the throbbing bruises forming on my backside.

"Please, just wait!" the guard yells, his voice further than before. *Did he stop?*

I glance back, but no, he hasn't stopped. My fall simply gained me a small lead. But not for long, as he's practically *skating* down the mountainside.

I dash the rest of the way until I'm on level ground. My strides gain confidence. I am, after all, an expert at running and hiding at this point. But he's at my heels faster than a flame spreading across brush. I push myself harder, muscles burning and still worn from last night's run.

But just as I'm drawing my dagger to fight, his fingers knot against my back. My momentum catches like a fish on a hook, and I'm jerked backward. My weight knocks against his, hard enough to break his balance, and we fall as one unit to the ground. I feel a puff of his humid breath in my hair, but his grip on me failed along with his stability. I rise and shove my boot against his throat before he can recover. My heel digs in until his eyes bulge, my glare and dagger threatening to kill him right here, right now.

"What do you want with me?" I demand.

His blazing gold eyes meet my mine, and a heaviness expands in my core.

The apprentice?

I almost jerk my boot away before I realize where we are and how far that is from where we'd last met.

Then his kindness was only a ruse.

"*What* do you want from me?" I repeat, heel sinking against his throat.

"Just wanted to talk," he squeaks beneath my boot. He gives my foot a light shove, far weaker than I can tell he's capable of—a *request* more than a threat to start another tussle with me.

I leave my boot where it is. "Then talk."

"Would rather do that without your boot in my throat."

"Then talk quickly, so I may decide whether or not to remove it."

He smiles, the most offensive thing he's done so far. "Are you lost?"

"Do I look lost?"

He stares at me, and I realize the stupidity of my question.

"I know exactly where I'm going, thank you," I say. "The better question is are *you* lost?"

"Figuratively."

My head tilts, and I almost forget I'm supposed to be threatening him. I shake off my curiosity and sharpen my glower. "Well, what are you doing out here? Following me?"

His fingers thrum the side of my boot. "Sort of a long story. Better told when I can breathe."

"I don't care about your story," I lie. "I want your reason. Tell me why you are following me."

He looks away, almost shy and I tense, unsure if it's part of the act or genuine. "I came looking for you because I knew you were in danger. That necromancer will come back as soon as the sun sets."

"*Noble.*" I fill my voice with doubt, despite the flutter in my chest. "And why are you out this way to begin with? Have you been following me since Fenfyre?"

"Thought you didn't want my story."

My heel sinks into his throat again.

He grabs my boot, this time pushing against my resistance. "You know I could reverse this real quick, don't you?"

"I doubt it."

I brace for his attempt, but instead, the humor washes from his face. "I'm from that town." His eyes flick toward the distance. I don't look. I remember seeing it well enough. My map had failed to tell me I was just a sprint from shelter last night. "I was going home to see my family."

"How very convenient." I narrow my gaze. "The smith you worked for didn't strike me as the type to care about such sentiments. Somehow, I find it hard to believe he would offer you the time off."

His lips twitch. "Oh, he insisted I take time off. Forever."

I gasp, guilt immediately retracting my foot. "I got you fired?"

He sits, rubbing the red sole imprint I left on his throat. My pulse throbs in his pause, another layer of guilt strapping itself around my shoulders. How is it that everyone I get anywhere close to finds misfortune because of it?

"No, I'd say, I got me fired," he says, voice hoarse from my aggression. "You're not the first person I cut a deal to. Grandfather didn't care for that."

My dagger sinks back into its sheath. *Grandfather? He's related to that wretched man?*

"So there. That's the story." He stands and brushes the dirt off his pants. "I sold you those arrows. Lost my job for it. I came back home and saw you out there running from the necromancer. I was worried you were lost, so I came looking."

"Seems you should be looking for a job, not a stranger," I say.

He rustles his hair, casting his gaze far from me. So *trusting*. Or am I that unintimidating to him?

"Well, one thing felt more urgent than the other," he answers. "Especially knowing a necromancer is after you. What are you doing way out here in the desert, anyway?"

"Hunting."

He studies my face like he's inspecting every brushstroke of a painting. My fingers twitch. If he recognizes who I am, the reward for turning me in would well cover the loss of his job, I'm sure. Not to mention the high honors the queen would place upon him.

Yet, his innocent smile begs me to question if he's even capable of having such a thought—even if he did suspect who I am.

"No one travels to the *desert* to hunt," he says with a laugh. "Really, what are you doing? Maybe I can help."

"I think you've gotten yourself into enough trouble helping me," I say, suddenly feeling like my chest plate is strapped too tight. "Don't let me cause you any more. You have a job to find. A family to get back to. I'll be fine. Thank you for all you've done. And I'm sorry for…everything."

I step toward the mountain where I left my belongings, but my feet drag. Once, twice, now three times I've had an opportunity to ask this man to aid me. Am I really going to let this slip by again? What's the worst that happens? He turns on me, and I have to wound him to escape?

No—the worst that happens is he *agrees*. Then he comes to the canyon with me to die like Verik.

I walk on, making it a few paces up the mountain slope before he calls after me.

"You're going to the canyon, aren't you?"

I freeze, the mountain before me blurring in my vision. I draw a slow breath before turning back with a strained chuckle. "That monsters' den? Who in the lands would do that?"

His stoic expression wipes the smile off my face.

"A descendant of Athenias Seraphine," he says.

All my extremities numb. I stare into his unsteady gaze, mouth incapable of forming a response. All this way, and finally someone has recognized me—

Yet why is he looking at me like I'm the first sunrise after an age of darkness?

"That's who you are, isn't it?" He steps toward me, but his hands are down, posing me no threat. "You're an heiress to the Light."

My throat clenches, attempting to dam the truth inside—to protect him from where I sense this going. But a single word slips through, reeled free by my desperation to not do this alone.

"Yes."

For a second, his face remains flat, like he didn't hear me at all. Then he laughs, a short and shocked sound.

I strengthen my voice. "I am what you say, a descendant of Athenias. An heiress to the Light."

He covers his face with both hands, muffling a laugh with his palms before he rakes his fingers through his hair. "You're really going to the *canyon*?" His tone hits a higher octave.

"Yes."

He spins, blundering several steps away, where he supports himself against the mountainside like he's going to fall over from laughing. But he hardly sounds amused—more like he's cracked open and about to cry instead.

"To claim the Light?" he asks, an unhinged look on his face.

I fold my arms, squeezing myself tight. "Yes, we've established that."

He casts his gaze to the distance. His wide smile makes me feel guilty for getting his hopes up.

"Just because I'm going doesn't mean anything," I say. "I have no power to fight the netherbeasts until I am anointed, as you may have noticed. So, truly, there's little chance—"

"What if I helped you?" he cuts in.

Acid crawls into my throat. I tilt my head to the skies, groaning from the depths of my soul. I should have run. Why did I say any-thing?

"You can't fight netherbeasts," he continues. "But I can. Maybe we still don't make it, but we could at least *try*."

"No." Fear shrieks between my ears. "It's too dangerous. I shouldn't be doing this at all, let alone bringing someone else along. It's suicide. A waste. We're not getting past the beasts in the canyon. They're not like the necromancer. They're bigger. Giants—"

"I know." He waves his hands like he's clearing away fog. "I *know* what's in there. But if you're really the heiress, I can't just let you go alone." He marches toward me, something wild in his gaze that steals my breath. "I don't care what's in the way, if you can claim that Light and do something about this mess our kingdom's in, then let me come. I'll help you through the canyon. I'd help you through ten of them."

His excitement curls my faith like leaves deprived of sunlight. "We'll *die*. I can't—"

"I'm not afraid to die," he says with the firmness of a soldier.

"*I can't* handle the burden of another person's life being threat-ened on my account."

I turn, thinking I'll attempt another flight.

"You aren't asking me to do this," he says, and I balk. "I'm telling you I am. If I die, it's because of my decision."

I stiffen. His words feel so foreign. So unlike the conversations I had with the last man who aided me on this quest. *I'm doing this for you. If I die, it's for you.* Those were the words Verik often spoke, but so sweetly, I never knew how much they'd sting when I lost him.

"Vaeryn, I'm serious. Queen Solalé killed my mother for being one of the Faithful. She'd kill me too if she found me," he says, tilting to meet my downcast gaze. "I'll do anything to see an Illuminarch return. *Anything*."

I rub my temples, frowning as the miserable reality unfolds be-fore me. *He's right.* This is about more than me and my feeble heart. It's about reaching the Light and redeeming our kingdom from the netherworld. And if bringing him along gives me even a fraction more of a chance, I have to allow it.

For the kingdom's sake.

I release a defeated sigh. "The portal is near the center of the canyon, east of the river. My father's map will lead us right to it. But, as I said, I have no power until I'm anointed by the Light. And in such a shadow-laden place, we cannot expect the sunlight to offer more than a few hours of protection even at day. Our survival will be entirely up to how fast we can run and how well you fight."

The wildness calms from his eyes, his lips straightening into a firm line. "I'll get you to the portal."

"You have much experience fighting netherbeasts, then?"

"The necromancer," he says.

Graces.

"You didn't touch him, only his pack. That hardly counts."

His gaze flicks to the side. "I also spent six years at the Bronze Guard Academy training under the most highly esteemed masters in the kingdom. They wanted to recruit me out of smithing to join the guard because I could best most of my peers." He runs his hand across the bow on his back. "Also, I've been shooting one of these since I was three. Think I'll figure it out in there."

I hardly hear any of his credits after his "no." Training in the academy is one thing, fighting real netherbeasts—real monsters—is another thing altogether. But Verik wasn't much different. In his few months of training, he only fought a couple of netherbeasts before we set out to cross the kingdom, yet I didn't count him out.

"What is your name?" I ask.

The zeal in his eyes nearly makes me nauseous. "Ezro Valorian."

"Well then, Ezro Valorian," I say, dread thinning my voice. "It seems you've found yourself a job after all."

11
EZRO

"We can ride it to Rōsrun," I say, adding Vaeryn's bag to my terraglider's storage compartment. ōProbably as far as we can take it unless we want the queen to sense where we're going. I'll trade it in for a boat there."

Vaeryn stares at the glider, sucking her bottom lip. I try not to imagine her crowned and draped in royal clothes—the way she should and would be if not for Solalé usurping Illuminarch Athenias—but I can't help it now. How did the heir to the kingdom cross paths with me? How does she even exist after all these years?

And what am I doing, thinking I can keep her alive?

Her gaze returns to me, the brilliant blue of her irises lit like the morning sky. "Wouldn't you like to tell your family where you're going first?"

I still, all my excitement settling like shed leaves across the cracked foundation of my being. "No. They don't exactly want to see me again."

Vaeryn gives me a puzzled look.

"Let's just say my visit didn't go well." I rub the back of my neck.

"They're on Solalé's side, anyway. I'm not sure I trust them to know who you are, what we're doing."

"Ah," is all she says after a long moment of thought.

I swoop my leg over my terraglider and stand, waiting for her, but she doesn't budge.

"Afraid to ride?" I ask.

"No." She steps forward. "I've ridden one before."

My brows scrunch, and I wonder if it's fear of the rider, not the vehicle, that's slowing her down. But finally, she swings herself into position behind me, and we sit. Her warmth emanates from the small gap between us and sinks through my leather armor. My first passenger.

And she's the future Illuminarch.

"Rōsrun is a bit of a ride from here," I say, hands tingling with nerves. *What if I crash? What if I get her discovered in Rōsrun? What if we don't even make it to the canyon to find out whether I really can handle the monsters within?* "We should be there before sundown. Can you stay at an inn?"

Her voice slips over my shoulders. "Under a different surname and in the company of an apparent Bronze Guard, it shouldn't be a problem for the night."

I nod and send the energy from the crescent on my wrist to the terraglider, awakening its power.

"You're sure you don't want to think about this first?" Vaeryn asks before I can launch us forward.

"What's there to think about?" I run my finger against the smooth, metal throttle. "I could doubt you're telling the truth, but why would you risk your life telling someone marked with the crescent a lie like that? I could sit around debating if it's worth the risk, and in the meantime, people like us are being hanged in the capital and towns are ravaged by netherbeasts. Yeah, what you're telling me sounds crazy, but most things that change the world are. Think I'd rather chance it than let you run into that canyon, alone, without a weapon that can even touch your enemies."

A hint of her sigh tickles my hair. "Adrenaline has a way of making us braver than we should be."

"Good thing it's not likely to wear off where we're going."

A large piece of debris in the path slows my glider to a standstill near the top of a hill. I squint at the corroded wood panels held by rusted nails to a snapped bracket. *A fence.* Or part of one.

A heaviness fills my chest as I scour the arid slope for more. I spot another scrap near a green mesquite tree, a crow perched on its sun-rotted boards. I frown, throttling the terraglider up the hill. When we reach the top, I brake again, jaw falling at the sight below. Wrecked buildings lie in ruin inside what remains of the devastated fence. Shattered glass glares in the sunlight, like stars dropped into the desert. And in the midst of it, the only thing standing upright is a bronze statue of Queen Solalé with her arms stretched toward the sky. Her shrine. The only thing the netherbeasts didn't destroy.

"Please tell me this isn't Rōsrun," Vaeryn says, leaning around me to see.

"It's Dunas," I say, my old neighbors' faces flashing through my mind. I can still hear the weary weeping that announced their arrival in Jarden. "Their steward refused to mandate the ceremonies honoring the queen. So she withdrew the Bronze Guard and let the netherbeasts have them. The few that survived are in Jarden now."

"*Graces.*"

My gaze lowers to my glider's handlebars. *This could still happen to Jarden. Even without me there to increase the odds.*

I shove the thought away, remembering who my passenger is. The heiress. If there's anything I can do to save my family—whether they deserve it or not—it's *this.* Helping the Illuminarch's descendant reach the realm of her anointing. Giving her a fighting chance against the netherworld.

"Be watchful," Vaeryn says. "I've passed many ruins along my way. They often aren't as abandoned as they may—"

A loud *clank* twists our attention behind. I spot a long metal chain falling from the back of my glider. Just as I notice the hook, another snags the side of the vehicle. I clutch the throttle, hoping my glider will overpower the bond. Instead, my glider leaps upward, then jerks to the right, throwing us both to the ground.

My pauldron smacks the hard desert floor, buffering the impact. I jump to my feet and snatch my bow and arrow, but Vaeryn's already shooting before I can draw the string. Her arrow flies across the debris, piercing the archer's arm the very second that he reemerges to try again. My brows raise. *So that's* what she needed those for.

"Bandits," she whispers, readying another arrow.

Gathered that.

A loud scraping noise twists me the other way—my glider, packed with our supplies, being dragged by the chains.

"Bet you would like to have that," I say, tracing the line until I spot a pair of rugged hands towing it from behind a wall-like boulder. I shift to pursue the thief, but the hum of steel averts my attention to a swordswoman racing from her covering. Her longsword glints in the high sun as she lifts her weapon, fearlessly exposing her steel-plated body. I glide my aim to the small opening between her full-face helmet and chest plate, but my hand stalls with the realization she'll die if I release my arrow.

A metallic hiss sings over my hesitation, and a second later, Vaeryn's sword collides with our enemy's. I scowl at myself, realizing my error. I should have swapped weapons, too. I trade my bow for my staff and turn my attention to the terraglider just as it's pulled behind the large boulder.

I chase after, blades clanging behind me. Somehow, I trust that Vaeryn doesn't need my help. But what she *does* need is her map, which is soon to be looted and likely used for fire kindling.

I approach the boulder, staff ready to jab the man behind it when another bandit charges me from the side. I swivel my heel, barring my staff to block his sword. All my training with Sterling comes alive inside my body, moving me thoughtlessly as I parry his next two strikes and land an air-stealing hit to his thinly armored chest. He fumbles back, only for his ally to forsake my glider and rise to his defense.

My staff vibrates as I thwart his swipe toward my throat, then whooshes to block another blow from my original opponent. For several measured breaths, I bar their attacks with stiff twists of my staff, calculated as the hands of a clock. Then I stake my staff and use it to propel a harsh kick to one's chest. The man blunders, sparing his balance for but a second before I spin back the other way and heel-kick him to the ground.

My focus snaps to my other opponent, who stands aback with his sword raised in defense. I squeeze the leather grips on my staff and charge. With a burly yell, he runs to meet me, but just a few paces before we collide, I plant my staff into the ground and use it to vault myself over his head. My boots slam the earth behind him, and he whirls to face me, just in time for my staff to bash him in the fore-head. His eyes roll, and he topples to the dirt.

For now.

I shift toward the bandit I'd kicked over, but the moment our eyes meet, he shakes his head and runs.

I watch him until he disappears behind the rubble then turn my attention to the other side of the fight. The female bandit is curled on the ground, moaning, and well beyond her, Vaeryn is fighting two bandits with a dagger in one hand and a short sword in the other. My feet pivot to aid her, but I fail to move, entranced by her skill to wield both weapons at once. *Who taught her that?*

I'm just shaking from my daze to help when Vaeryn sneaks a jab into one of their underarms. The bandit yowls as blood seeps through his armor. The next second, Vaeryn is behind the other ban-dit with her sword pressed to his throat and the tip of her dagger poking his abdomen.

"Drop your weapon," she orders.

The man's sword clamors to the rocky ground. Vaeryn kicks it, sending it sliding beneath a collapsed wall. The wounded bandit weakly draws his weapon, taking one step before he notices me watching. His sword returns to his sheath, and he flees, forsaking his ally.

"Make any attempt to follow us, and we will not be so merciful," Vaeryn says to the bandit in her possession.

She meets my gaze expectantly, and after a moment, I register her silent order. I trade back to my bow and arrow, holding a threat toward the bandit so she can step away freely. She marches toward me, face splotched in red and panting, but despite our victory, her gaze is low.

I backstep toward my terraglider, an arrow still pointed at the bandit while Vaeryn checks our supplies. Once she deems everything in place, we mount and blaze past the wreckage of Dunas.

12

EZRO

We reach Rōsrun just as the sunset is touching the two-story rooftops. I pull to a stop outside the green-speckled copper gate, and Vaeryn and I dismount the glider. I guide it toward the guards, Vaeryn following like a shadow with her chin tucked toward her collarbone.

"Passing through," I say.

"Welcome, sir," the older Bronze Guard says, eyeing the crescent on my breastplate. His gravelly voice reminds me of Grandfather's. That same bitter, worn out, had-enough-of-everything drone that attempts to sound friendly despite. "Haven't seen your face before. What barracks are you coming from?"

"Fenfyre. One of Sterling's," I say, hoping the use of my academy trainer's notable name will make it more convincing.

"Ah," is all he says, but at the moment I expect him to turn and unlatch the gate, his attention switches to Vaeryn. "Who'd you bring with you?"

My mouth hangs. Lies never come easy to me. *A friend? A trainee? No, she'd have the mark—*

The man's eyes narrow at her, then a smile transfigures his face. "That'll do, dear," he says to her.

I glance back to see what in the lands he's talking about just in time to see her stuffing a necklace back under her shirt. The fleeting glimpse is enough to catch the wind in my lungs. Moonstone pendant. Crescent charm dangling over it. *A marriage token.* To a Bronze Guard.

As in *me.*

She could have warned me we were going with that before we got here.

The metal lock snaps, jerking my attention to the guard. The gate creaks open and the other guard steps forward to collect my terraglider and adds it to the half-dozen others sitting idle within the gate. *Right. Narrow walkways.*

"Welcome in," the older guard says, but I hardly get to fake a smile at him before a hand latches onto mine. Instinct almost launches me into defense before I realize whose hand it is and why. It's Vaeryn's. For the sake of our deception.

Well, this is going to be fun. I've never even held a girl's hand that wasn't my mother's or my sister's, and now I'm pretending to be married to the future Illuminarch.

I give her hand a firm squeeze; not enough to hurt, but enough to tell her I'm not happy and she will hear about this the first chance I get.

We step into a small city I haven't seen since my youth. Its uneven brick streets and two-story shops don't impress me like they did before I saw Fenfyre, but what it has that Fenfyre lacked is the beautiful river running straight through the middle. It's lined by a stout brick fence with elegant sconces sleeping on each pier, and all across the town are arched wood bridges. One squeaks as I lead Vaeryn over it and toward the lazy market.

I hang onto her hand as we walk—half because I'm not sure if it will ruin our façade if I recoil from her, and half because I want to see how long she'll tolerate it. Which is approximately ten more steps. Then she lets go, wipes her hand off *twice*, and shrugs at me. I scowl and glance around to be sure no other Bronze Guards are nearby to overhear me.

"Might have been nice if you'd warned me about your plan first," I say.

"I assumed the plan was obvious." There's the faintest flush on her cheeks, but whether for the heat, embarrassment, or annoyance, I can't tell. "We bear no resemblance. I figured you'd come up with the same idea."

"Not an expert at deceit. Sort of disappointed that you are, considering…" *Who you are.*

She marches past me. "I haven't had much choice. And if you had a better—more *honest*—means of getting me inside, then perhaps you should have spoken up quicker."

I lengthen my strides to keep up with her. "Where'd you get that, anyway?"

"Off a dead body," she says under her breath.

My imagination replays the fatal intensity she'd fought those bandits with. "Like someone you made dead?"

I expect her to laugh at my partial joke. Instead, her eyes avert mine and her words harden like freshly quenched steel. "Not directly."

"How do you indirectly kill someone?"

"Not as complicated as it might sound," she says. "This is not an in-the-city conversation."

I glance at the few people scattered around us. Everyone seems preoccupied by something. A child. A dog. A heavy load they're carting somewhere. I leave it alone for now and scan the buildings for the inn. I spot it right off the river, overlooking the dock, and lead us on. But only once we're approaching the check-in desk inside do I realize the other consequence of Vaeryn's lie. No one will believe we are married if I ask for separate rooms.

The attendant flutters her quill, looking between us. "Names, please."

"Ezro and Vaeryn Valorian," I say, grimacing at the sound of this stranger wearing *my* last name. Even worse, it sounds nice when I say it. Like the name suits her better than it does me.

"Very well," she says, jotting our names in her record book. "One night?"

"Yes."

The attendant bobs her head as she writes a room number. A sweat forms on my neck as she grabs a single key and sets it down, just out of my reach. *Guess I'm sleeping on the floor.*

"Excuse me," Vaeryn cuts in. The attendant's eyes bat with a flair of annoyance. "Do you have two rooms available? I have trouble enough sleeping whilst traveling, and his snoring makes it near impossible."

The woman chuckles. "A bit young to be annoyed with him already, hmm?" She looks across the pages. "Yes, I have a few rooms left. If it's worth the coin to you."

Vaeryn's gaze flicks toward me.

"Yes," I say, pulling out my coin sack faster than I should.

The woman slants her head.

"He's tired of getting elbowed in the ribs," Vaeryn covers. Her laugh smooths the attendant's face back out.

From now on, she talks to people.

We close the transaction and receive our keys.

The next morning, we divide our efforts in the market to shop for supplies. I send Vaeryn with a healthy sack of coin to buy herself some decent clothes while I focus on food and other necessities. I carefully select from Rōsrun's abundance until the sun is glaring over the shingled rooftops. Then I turn for the apparel store to check on Vaeryn, but four steps shy of the door, it swings open.

First thing I see is a mound of clothes wadded in someone's arms. Then I recognize that "someone" as a freshly clothed Vaeryn. She smiles at me the same way I used to smile at Niah when I'd done something wrong on her watch.

"For as hard as it was to get you to *take* my money, you sure had no problem spending it," I say. "Think that's all gonna fit in a boat?"

She lets the clothes sag in her arms so I can see her entire face and all of its annoyance. "It's not all mine. Half of this is *yours*."

"You bought *me* clothes?"

"You bought you clothes. I just picked them out. Not promising they'll fit." Her nose points toward the river. "Are we done here? I'd like to get out of this town while the day is young."

I almost ask to look at the clothes first to be sure they'll fit, but the impatience in her eyes turns my feet toward the docks.

I hand the boater the money I earned selling my terraglider, and the boater motions us toward the canoe of Vaeryn's choosing. We tuck our supplies into the compartments under the seats and climb aboard while the boater unhitches the river gate. The canoe tugs at its tether, like the water is calling to it, and as soon as the boater unhooks it, the current sweeps us forward.

13

EZRO

"Let's stop here," Vaeryn says after several hours on the river.

The sunset paints the water gold, like a stream of honey rolling between the tall trees around us. Vaeryn coaxes the canoe toward land and latches it to a sturdy tree before she climbs out. The boat teeters as I stand, legs aching from the long sit. I wobble onto the ground and scan the premises. The evergreens perfume the air with a pungent scent that stings my nose. The occasional cactus nestles between their reddish barks, little reminders of home. Those will disappear soon, I'm sure. Soon nothing will be familiar anymore but the feeling of my weapons in my hands.

"I'm going to gather firewood before the sun goes down," I say after we've unloaded the boat.

Vaeryn eyes the position of the sun. "That leaves little time. I will help."

I turn into the woods, wandering until I find a treasure trove of firewood: a collapsed tree. I snap off a brittle limb and toss it to start a pile. Vaeryn approaches the tree, but her gaze skates around the area like she's looking for some place away from me that might offer

78

equal promise. When she doesn't see it, she kicks one limb three times until it breaks loose.

The sight is so unexpectedly brutal in these serene woods that I have to remind myself to move again.

"So, where exactly are you from?" I ask.

"Brïsbrook," she says, heel snapping a branch off the broken limb.

"Brïsbrook? What have you been traveling for, months?"

"Six." Another branch cracks under her foot.

"Alone?"

She tosses the two branches into the pile, avoiding looking at me, even though I'm standing right beside it. "That wasn't the original plan, but that's how it's gone, yes."

I copy her method, stomping on the decaying tree. It rattles and snaps under my boot. "Should I ask what happened?"

"Probably not."

My head tilts, and I expect her to leave it there. Instead, she returns to assault the tree again. A loud pop, then, "When I was a girl, my father raised me with one expectation: as soon as I came of age, he would set out for the Etherium to claim the Light. He chose to wait until I was grown, knowing the likelihood of his success was slim. He'd lost his father as a boy to this quest, and he wanted me old enough to handle the loss of my father should it come to it."

She carries her next branch over, stopping to meet my curious gaze. She stalls, studying me a moment before looking away again. "However, not long before my eighteenth birthday, my father was attacked by an elderwolf pack. He was rescued, but the wolves shredded his left leg, crippling him for the rest of his life. After this, my father asked my older brother, Liander, to go in his place."

"But?" I ask when she pauses.

"Liander is a coward. He refused the responsibility." She returns to her branch, giving it a harsh kick.

"So your father sent you?"

She releases a solemn laugh, shaking her head. "When Liander refused, my father decided to take the journey anyway. My mother convinced him to wait another year to regain some strength, and in that time, I began my own preparations with the help of a friend. My parents both rejected the idea of me going—given my resemblance to my great-grandmother, not to mention their other doubts. The night before my father was to set out, I stole his map and ran off with my friend in secret."

"And your friend...?" I ask, clinging to a stick I meant to toss minutes ago.

"Dead."

Her answer hits with the finality of a closed door. I quell my curiosities about it and pick a less personal question to save the conversation with. "How has your family survived all this time?"

She sets back to work on her branch, slower than before. "As far as I know, we're the only remnant of the lineage. My great-grandmother, the last Illuminarch, had two sons. One died with the Luminors, the other—my grandfather—feigned his death and went into hiding with his fiancé. They married, had my father in secret, and by the time I was born, enough time had passed that we could live somewhat integrated into society. But of course, only if we maintained a perfect veil of lies."

"So it's a miracle you're alive, then."

She smiles. "In more ways than one."

I catch my gaze lingering on her softened features, and turn, tossing my stick into the pile. "So, how did Solalé manage to defeat the Luminors?"

She takes in a long, slow breath. "She didn't."

My head jerks back. "What?"

"There are two netherwitches in Paran'dan. Solalé is the lesser of the two."

My brows pinch. *Netherwitches? Two?*

Vaeryn continues before I can ask. "The stronger is what's known as a witchlord, a ruler of the netherworld. He's the one who defeated the Luminors—all but one." Her stare turns distant, as if recalling a memory rather than facts. "My great-grandmother fought him and was nearly overpowered. With the last of her vitality, she created a prison of pure light, trapping him inside it. But Solalé was waiting in the wings. The moment Illuminarch Athenias fell, she stole the throne."

My hands flail in front of me. "Wait. Hold on. I've never even heard of a netherwitch."

"They didn't teach you in the academy?"

"No."

"*Figures.*" She leans her back against a tree, staring up at the orange sky. "They are the highest-ranking beings in the netherworld. Little is really known about how extensive their power is or the specifics of it, but Father did say that while their physiological powers are dangerous, their psychological ones are even worse. Some can read minds, search memories. Father believed some have an ability to overcome one's own will. The witchlords are the most powerful of them all." She suddenly looks toward the dimming sun, tone switching as if we were merely discussing the turn of the season. "We're losing light. We need to get back. This should be plenty."

I fail to move. "What if he got out?"

"No telling, but I'm sure it would be nothing short of turning this world into an extension of the netherworld," she says. "But a century has passed, and he remains bound. Either Solalé is pleased with this, or she's incapable of releasing him. It's her we need to worry about for now. Come on."

I gather the kindling, and we reach our campsite with enough sunlight left to build our fire before the sky dyes a velvety black. Vaeryn and I sprawl our blankets on opposite sides of the fire, as far apart as we can safely be, and assemble our belongings to our liking. We exchange a few awkward, distant glances. The kind that are obviously checking for the same thing. *Are you watching me?*

I leave my blanket and finagle a branch so it reaches over the campfire—a trick Father taught me on our hunting trips. Retrieving a small steel kettle from my bag, I fill it with river water and affix it to the prop stick. Vaeryn wanders over and sits in the firelight with her knees bent toward her chin. Her gaze follows my hands as I prepare two of Father's camping cups with tea. One with chamomile for her, and one with black leaf to keep me awake. I tuck the tea tins away, and Vaeryn's stare moves to the fire, lids slowly drooping as the fire dances in the darks of her eyes. There's so much more I want to ask her—like she's a history book just waiting to be opened. But one that holds the truth—the whole of it—which has been denied the rest of us all this time.

But I'd have to be as heartless as my grandfather to keep prodding her right now for how exhausted she looks. Besides, I can already feel the snake of self-doubt slithering up my spine the darker it gets out here. I don't need her conscious to see me sweat when it constricts me.

I snatch the kettle as soon as it whistles and pour it over the tea leaves. After a few minutes of steeping, I chuck the wet leaves from their strainers and extend Vaeryn's cup to her, but the only thing that lifts toward it is her heavy gaze.

"Don't like tea?" I ask.

She hesitates another moment before grabbing it.

We sip the tea with our attention latched onto the fire. The wood crackles as the flames chew away at the bark, dropping burning cinders that fade to ash against the dirt. The smoke has a warmer scent than the fire in the forge, and the way it mixes with the aroma of my tea reminds me of late nights by a bonfire with Niah. But it's missing the feeling of home. Of *her.*

Or who I thought she was. The thought poisons my stomach.

Vaeryn stirs from her fire-watching trance to look at me. "We'd be wise to take shifts. Shall I take the first?"

I'm almost surprised she's *asking* and not telling me how things are going to be. "No, I'll take the first watch."

She sets her cup aside. "You're sure you'll last a few more hours?"

"Sure. Got tea and plenty to worry about." I smile. "Shouldn't be a problem."

A pause settles between us before her exhaustion persuades her to take my offer. "Well, holler at me if you change your mind." She walks toward her blanket but jerks her gaze back to me before she reaches it. "And Ezro, if you come near me while I'm asleep, I'll send you to the Elysium."

A laugh puffs from my nose. "Stay away from me, and I'll stay away from you."

She lays down with her back to me, hiding herself entirely within her cloak. I stare at her shrouded form, both burdened and purposed by who she is and the reality that the only thing standing between her and death is me. I grab my bow, already feeling a sweat forming on the back of my neck.

And that's when the noises begin—guttural and hollow noises rolling through the woods like stampedes of ghosts.

14

VAERYN

Blood. Blood is all I see as I run to Verik.

It's pouring from slits in his neck. Seeping through tears in his leather armor. Staining the snow beneath him.

It sprays me when he coughs—hot droplets across my face.

His weak grip wraps around my arms and pulls me closer. The fog of his labored breath clouds the mere inches between us, and my trembling heart prepares to hear the words I always wanted him to say, delivered in his last chance to speak them.

We're lucky to have this moment. Had dawn not broken and the sun not spilled over the hill, the bearish netherbeast would have finished him too soon. I wouldn't have been able to make it to his side, to spend his last moments with him. To hear him say, "I love you."

But those aren't the words that gargle from his lips.

"Go," he says instead. A bitter, wretched sound. "Go claim the Light."

"I can't." My words are fainter than his, as if I'm the one fading, not him. "I can't make it there without you."

"Then what am I dying for, Vaeryn?"

An icy tear drops off my chin into the blood smeared on his cheek. "Verik, I—"

"Go!"

His demand pierces like a spear through my lungs. *Angry. He's so angry. At me. This is my fault—*

I open my lips to apologize, to promise I'll go to any length to make his death mean something, to tell him I've loved him more than anyone besides my father. But his grip on my arms fails, hands thudding the snow. His eyes turn up. Empty. Soulless. No cloud escapes his lips. And it's too late. He'll never hear it. He'll never know.

I didn't even say goodbye.

The scream that escapes my lips is worse than any sound I've heard. Worse than the shriek of every netherbeast combined.

But when my eyes open from it, I feel the warmth of sunlight. It beams in beautiful rays between the trees, trees unlike the snow-dappled oaks Verik died between. These are tall spires, reaching into a stormless sky. And behind me is the soft chortle of a dying campfire, which jogs my consciousness back to where I really am. Not in the Tristlewood Forest where I lost Verik, but in the warm woodlands just south of the Creator's Canyon.

I sit, pushing my hood off my head. My fingertips wipe the sleep from my eyes before I look about the camp for my new companion, but I find his spot vacant.

A surge of panic lifts me to my feet. I spin, checking every angle once more to be sure I didn't miss him.

He's gone.

What have I done? Something must have come for me, and he tried to run it off. Now he's dead. Graces. This is all my fault.

I bolt in a random direction. "Ezro?"

My shout startles a few birds.

"Ezro!"

The blood rushing in my ears is louder than the river. I should have never agreed to this. I should have forced him to go home and leave me to my fate. I can't be responsible for—

"What? What's wrong?"

The back of my hand whisks my forehead, and I wheel around, squinting at the sunrise. Ezro emerges through the morning rays as if imparted by the sun itself. He steps into the shadow of a tree; the shade diffuses the light so I can see his purple under-eyes and heavy blinks.

"Vaeryn, what's wrong?" he asks again.

I try to allay the frantic pounding of my heart. "Nothing… Nothing is wrong. I just…"

A slanted grin swivels onto his lips. "You thought a netherbeast stole off with me."

"Something akin to that."

He looks me over, like he's trying not to laugh. "Nope. You didn't get that lucky. I'm still here. Just wanted to leverage that tree for some firewood to take with us."

"No trouble with netherbeasts, then?" I ask.

"Lots of noise, but nothing came close to us." He hugs the bushel of sticks to his chest as he starts toward the camp. "How'd you sleep?"

"Fine, besides that we were supposed to be taking shifts. Why didn't you wake me?"

"Got a better idea." He stops to face me. The sunlight swathes his face in gold, lighting his irises like drops of spring honey. "I'll sleep on the boat part of the day while the netherbeasts aren't out. That way, we both get decent rest. Keep us moving too. I want to get there as fast as we can."

Ezro's plan seems brilliant until I discover his definition of "sleeping" seems to be lying awake, staring at the inner wall of the canoe with his face tensed like he's in terrible pain.

I rest the paddle. My arms are sore from battling through a rocky stretch. The way looks clear for now, and the current is polite here. I glance at Ezro to see if he's found rest yet, but find the same sight as the last three times I checked. Only this time, he notices me.

The stress lines smooth from his forehead. A smirk sparks his eyes from their grave trance, and he sits. "Useless," he says, raking his fingers through his hair. I watch each wavy clump find a new place above his brow. "Been lying here for two hours."

"Is it the boat?"

"No, it's me," he groans. "Can't sleep anywhere. Beds. Boats. Darkness. Daylight. Doesn't matter."

"It's not that we are approaching the canyon then, either?" I ask.

"I'm ready for the canyon." His voice is steady and sure. "Rather face things than dread them."

My chin lowers. The quickening in my pulse alerts me that I don't feel the same, though I wish I did. Six months questing for this. One life paid so far to get me here, and at the precipice, I'm shuddering inside.

"You're worried," Ezro says.

I wince, surprised by his notice. I open my mouth to attempt a trite denial, but his eyes convict me back into silence.

His gaze tilts down. "You never told me about that," he says, and I feel the cold pendant between my fingers.

I clutch it in my hand, hiding it. My stomach cramps. I'd hoped he'd forgotten, and now my fingers have fiddled it right back to the forefront of his mind.

I squint downstream, hoping to see some wild twists or protruding rocks—a distraction. No such blessing. The river is apparently more his friend than mine.

"Don't tell me it's a not-on-the-river conversation, too," he says.

My clutch on the pendant tautens, the chain digging into the back of my neck. Any tighter and I might break it. "It belonged to a friend."

There. *Tell me that's enough.*

His sneer vanishes. "The one who came with you?"

I nod.

He lowers his chin, looking at me with such genuine concern, I feel dizzy.

"What happened to her?"

Her. Oh, I can't handle this. My eyes look at the evergreens as our boat carries us by. I wet my lips to speak but don't find the words until they are dry again.

"Not *her.*"

His most subtle recoil imprints on my mind. Something I will ponder over later, when I'm not owning up to my hand in Verik's death.

"His name was Verik. He was a close friend of mine, so much so that I entrusted him with my family's secrets. He was passionate about seeing the Luminors return, and when he learned I was planning on traveling to the Etherium myself, he was eager to help me get there. He joined the Bronze Guard just to gain a mark like your own, since I couldn't do so without risking my true identity being discovered." My lungs feel deprived of air. How can this be the first time I'm having to say these things aloud? "He really believed he could protect me, despite his short training at the northern academy. It was only one month into our journey when netherbeasts overtook him."

Ezro is quiet for a while, his gaze lingering on the pendant. "You found that on him after."

Air stutters through my nose. "It all made sense then. Why he helped me."

"I'm sorry."

I press on a smile. "Thank you."

I hide the pendant beneath my top and check on our path. When I see it's still clear, my body sinks deeper into my seat—as if guilt had perched on each of my shoulders like iron-feathered ravens. Ezro's silence abandons me to the ravens' accusations. The never-ending "shoulds" and "shouldn'ts" that ravage my peace. And yet here I sit on a boat racing straight for the canyon to put another man at risk. *My* mission. *My* mantle. *My* responsibility.

All hinging on another's skill and survival.

"How have you kept alive since then?" Ezro asks.

My gaze lifts to the quivering trees. "After he died, the Illuminant began sending a spirit to me. Raphós. He dwells in the Etherium, but he's been given charge over the Luminors. He doesn't always make it, such as the other night. I'm not sure why that is. Either the Illuminant must deem it unnecessary, or perhaps he is delayed." A falcon's shadow sweeps across the canoe, deceiving me for a moment that Raphós appeared at the sound of his name. Not that calling it out has ever helped. "Regardless, Raphós is the main reason I'm still alive. Otherwise, I've survived by running. I managed well with that until I reached the desert. Everything is far more hostile out here. From the people and beasts to the weather."

His smile returns. "Yeah, we're a wicked lot, aren't we?"

Heat blossoms across my cheeks, but I don't find a response quick enough before he moves past it.

"What's the north like? Besides cold."

My muscles loosen, relaxing against the stern. "Lush. It rains almost every morning in Brïsbrook during spring and autumn. In summer, there are festivals and shows that go on for days, some for weeks, even. It's a quiet place otherwise, especially in winter. Then, sometimes there's too much snow to even get out the front door."

I keep talking, checking the river every so often to be sure it's still safe. His eyelids get heavier as he listens. I tell him every pleasant thing I can think of about home, from the fine breads to the feeling of sitting by the fireplace with a wool sweater to keep warm, reading the winter lore. When my words slow, he smiles at nothing specific and lies down.

My brows scrunch, unsure if I've bored him to sleep or if hearing about the north comforted him somehow. Whichever it is, he's lost in dreams the next minute.

I stare longer than I should, heart throbbing in my chest as I study his face. The old bruises on his ear and brow have nearly faded, much like his tension. A slight smile curves his lips, leaving me to wonder what sights fill his imagination now. Ones I painted? Pleasant memories of his own, stirred by my nostalgia? Or perhaps hopes of the days to come should we succeed in our mission?

I catch myself smiling back. "Precious" is the last word a man would want to be called, but it's the only word that surfaces in my head. But then I feel the pendant weighing on my neck—a constant reminder of Verik, of what my admiration cost another man.

I lift my gaze beyond Ezro and forbid myself to think of him in such a way again.

15

EZRO

"Wake up. We're here."

I stir, confused by who's talking before I register Vaeryn sitting at the stern, her blonde braid dangling over her shoulder. A gold-flecked sky sprawls overhead, alerting me I've been out for hours.

I sit, my entire body aching from the awkward way I'd lain in the boat. My head cranes back as I take in the rising red walls around us. They stand at least a mile from the river on each side, a west shadow nearly touching the water.

"I want to pull off so we can find a place to camp before sundown," Vaeryn says.

"That was fast," I say, a fresh wind of nerves tickling through my ribs at the thought of night in the canyon.

"The river picked up quite a bit. White water, even. It's a wonder you slept through it." She pauses her paddling to smile at me. "I was afraid I hadn't just bored you to sleep, but straight to death."

I flounder through my foggy memory until I remember what she means. I asked her about Brïsbrook, and five minutes into her talking about it, I couldn't keep my eyes open. But I'd rather not admit it had less to do with being bored and was more about the pleasant sound of her voice while she talked about it.

I grab my paddle. "Well, if we're getting out to camp, let's do it. The deeper in we go, the more dangerous. Let's ease into it."

"I thought you were ready to face it?" she teases, directing the canoe toward the shadow.

I help her steer it to the shore. "Doesn't mean I need to be dumb about it. I want to get a taste for what I'm up against first."

"Think of the necromancer, only ten times larger and some can disguise themselves into the landscape."

"Perfect."

She anchors the canoe, and we step out onto solid land. My legs quiver, and the ground seems to teeter like the river after the long ride. Even Vaeryn walks like she's disoriented, not that her face shows it. Her stoic expression reminds me of who she really is—someone people like me shouldn't be allowed to look at, let alone converse with.

The red-stained earth crunches under our boots, mottled with dried evergreen needles and pine cones. The trees are sparser than they were at our last camp, with more shrubs and dirt than anything. Not exactly what I was hoping for. I wanted as much foliage to hide us as possible—for what little good that might do.

We decide on a spot near the auburn canyon wall and lay out our campsite with the bare necessities just in case we need to bolt. Once we've settled everything, we sit beside our fire, silently fill our stomachs, and sip tea. When Vaeryn is done, she stretches her arms, probably sore from wrestling the currents all day, and stands. She scans the perimeter, which is dying gray from the falling sun.

"You're sure about this?" she asks. "We can still go back."

"To what? The way things have always been?" I sip the last of my tea and set the cup on a smooth stone. "What then? I go waste my life hammering steel in some random town where I don't know anybody? And you do what? Go back to Brïsbrook and pretend you're somebody else while your family's kingdom is suppressed by netherbeasts and the Illuminant's Faithful are hanged? Sounds like torture to me."

She shuffles back to the fire and sits. "It's like you were born for this," she says, her eyes not quite meeting mine.

More like broken for it.

"Maybe I was. Maybe we both were."

The sunlight dissolves into blackness, and the canyon awakens. Noises climb the walls, resounding in undetectable directions. Vaeryn lies down, the fall of darkness her cue to sleep under my watch. She rests closer than she did last night. Near enough that once she falls asleep, I can hear her soft breathing.

I hold my bow, an arrow ready in my other hand to be nocked and launched at the first sign of movement. But for hours, nothing comes. Just the groans and hisses and rumbles that raise goosebumps on my arms.

But we've barely breached the canyon. They're probably waiting for us to come to them.

Vaeryn rises just before the sun. She rolls, locating me before she draws her first waking breath. Then she sits, throws her hood back, and inspects the sky.

"Almost dawn," I whisper, nodding toward the pale light hinting over the canyon wall.

"Anything come by?" she asks.

"Nothing."

I feel her sigh as if I'd released it myself. Neither of us speaks or moves again until the sunlight prances into the ravine. My bones slacken at the feeling of the light against my skin. *Protection.* Another night done. How many will it take to get us to the Etherium?

"Can I see the map again?" I ask.

Vaeryn digs it from her bag and hands the rolled parchment to me. I unfurl it, laying it across my lap. Just east of the center of the canyon, there's an X marking the location of the portal. I study the hand-inked map, attempting to guess our location, then measure the distance with my fingers. It looks like the stretch of eternity knowing what lies between here and there, but with the river's help, it's maybe a week out.

Just a week. Seven nights in the monster-ridden canyon.

So, yeah. Eternity.

"What will the portal look like?" I ask, rolling the map.

Vaeryn takes it. "I have no idea. Father wasn't sure either. I'm hoping we'll know it when we see it."

"Yeah, probably by the number of netherbeasts guarding it."

She tucks the map into her bag. "Or the size of them."

I frown when her back turns. She wanders far from my view, returning only once I've loaded everything into the canoe. She's changed clothes, and her braid is damp, like she'd gone upstream to bathe. I realize I'd better do the same, and I abandon her for another twenty minutes. When I return, she's furiously scribbling in a journal.

"Writing a memoir?" I ask.

She jolts—good thing I wasn't a bear—and the pen flings into the dirt. The journal closes, and she scoops the pen up, stuffing both from my sight like she's offended I caught her with it.

"It's my personal records, thank you," she says, marching for the canoe.

I can't help but laugh. "So, a diary then."

"*Records.*"

I shake my head, musing at her insistence as we climb aboard the boat with me at the stern now that I've gotten the gist of it. I wait until we've settled in, and I've released the tether to make another comment. "My sister kept a diary, too. Back when she was *nine*."

She twists to give me a vile glare. "Well, if *you* were completely alone for five months, you'd want a place for your thoughts, too. Those pages have been my only friend through the hardest days of my life. I don't need your teasing over it."

I flinch, and she turns back around.

I watch her jagged motions, confused by how quickly the mention of her journal ignited her. *Stars.* I must have forgotten she had sensitivities the day she rammed her boot into my throat.

"Sorry," I say after the boat finds its rhythm on the water. "I spent six years talking to myself on my grandfather's roof. Probably looked a lot crazier."

She settles, laying the paddle down since the current is docile. "Don't tell me you didn't have any friends there?"

Her tone is somehow both judgmental and concerned at once.

"My grandfather kept me like a dog on a leash," I say. "He didn't like me talking to people around the town. Think he was afraid people would put ideas in my head. He liked it better when his voice was the only one I knew well."

"How in the lands did he get away with that?" I feel her gaze as it sweeps over me, as if to suggest I could have overpowered him.

"Because I let him." My voice dips. "Thought it was what I had to do to earn my sister a better life once I inherited everything from him."

Her lips part, and I watch the mist from the river dancing around her pale face. Pity looks pretty on her, but I'd rather she not wear it because of me.

"Doesn't matter now. It's over," I say, showing her the crescent mark on my wrist. "Got what I needed from that situation."

Her pitiful expression remains even when I smile at her. I wish she'd wipe it. Her eyes feel like they are unearthing my very soul from my body. And it feels so foreign—to be looked at and truly *seen*. It almost feels like she cares. But why should she? It's probably just in my head. Maybe this is how she normally looks at people, like she's sorry for them that they were ever born.

She's just shifting away when the boat jostles to the right, water sloshing over the edge. It splashes Vaeryn's side, drops splattering into my face. Vaeryn curls, ducking her head into her lap as the boat teeters in the other direction and another blast of chilly water showers us. I wipe my face, looking to the river, expecting to see rocks jutting from a white-capped current. But instead, I see *claws*—small chitinous claws gripping the rims of our boat and rocking it.

Riverwraiths.

I snatch the two halves of my staff, not bothering to assemble it. More claws grip the rim, pushing down until frothing water splashes in from every side. I whack the closest wraith to me, and it releases a hair-raising shriek. The small, shell-armored creature dips into the water, its lithe form wiggling back into the depths. But its family assails the boat with more fury, tipping and turning and shaking the canoe. I bash and swipe at their claws, wraith after wraith recoiling only for others to return. Their piercing cries ring in my ears, growing louder the harder I fight them.

Vaeryn tosses water from the boat with a bucket, but it seems pointless. For every bucketful she throws, another wave comes in.

We're going to sink. Then the riverwraiths will drag us through the river and bash us against rocks until we die. I've heard enough stories about them from the Bronze Guards.

The boat rams into a rock with a loud crack. I turn only quick enough to see the split wood in the bow before one half of my staff is nearly jerked from my hand. I whap the wraith away with the other half, and my eyes meet with Vaeryn's, exchanging a silent, "Now what?"

But then, just over her head, I spot it—our way out. A fallen tree hanging over the water. If one of us can grab it—

"Vaeryn!" I shout, pointing behind her.

She twists around, standing just in time to reach for it. Her hand snatches a branch, and she pulls herself high enough to grab another. The wood pops, a threat to snap. She ignores it, swiftly lifting herself so her legs hug the slanted trunk. I duck as the river drags me past her, stomach falling as I realize what I've just done: left her dangling on a precarious tree with me sinking into the river.

She screams my name as the river pulls me on.

"Vae—"

A claw raking against my calf whirls me back into the fight. I bat the riverwraiths, their screeches filling the skies. The water rises, soaking into my boots and up my pants. When I look back for Vaeryn, the curve in the river prevents me from seeing her or the tree I left her on. If she falls, will they race to drown her? If she doesn't, will more netherbeasts emerge from the shadows on land?

The water sloshes nearly to the rim of the canoe. I look for another way out—another tree, a branch, *anything*. But there's nothing even close. My pulse quickens, breaths hissing through my teeth.

The water in the boat is so heavy that I'm barely moving anywhere but down. I twist my staff together just as more riverwraiths slip over the rim, claws reaching for my legs. I swat them back, the reality pressing against my lungs. There's no escape. I can fight all I want, but there are too many, and I'm going down.

I'm going to die in this river, and Vaeryn will be completely alone in the canyon.

Something thuds against the boat. I swivel around, finding a grappling hook sunk into the lip of the canoe. I follow the line until I see Vaeryn's white-knuckled hands yanking the rope. Her heels dig into the earth, wrestling with the impossible weight of the boat. I knock back another riverwraith, tuck my staff away, and lunge for the hook.

"Stop pulling!" I yell.

As soon as she does, I tug the hook loose and grip it. I eye Vaeryn just before I jump into the water. Immediately, claws are coiling at my ankles. I kick them back as I swim, the mark on my wrist enabling the blows from my feet to affect them, too. Vaeryn tows at the rope, pulling it around a tree to help fight the resistance. Her strength alarms me for her size, but the riverwraiths' desperation to have me only adds to theirs. The tension between the two forces stretches my body, tugging my joints. Water slaps over my head and fills my mouth. I cough and gasp, only for the river to douse me again. The wraiths heave at my boots, nearly pulling them from my ankles. But finally, I knock against the shore. Vaeryn's hands alternate down the rope until she reaches me, then she pulls me from the water and tosses me sideways.

I plummet into the muddy ground, wraiths still hanging onto my heels. I kick them off and crawl forward on my elbows until I'm out of their reach, then I roll onto my side, coughing until my lungs clear.

"Stars, you're strong," is all my dumb mouth can think to say when I look at Vaeryn. "And fast."

She pants, eyes fixed on the river. "Our supplies."

My smile falls. I sit, staring at the water. It's deceitfully calm, not a wraith in sight. As if nothing at all had happened.

"Our boat," I groan.

A sharp noise bursts from Vaeryn's lips as she kicks the ground. Her fingers coil into her hair. Then she paces away from me like someone who's about to kill.

I look back at the river as she continues stomping around, grumbling to herself. Morning shadows still blanket the water, despite the brilliant sky. I rise, stepping back to its edge. From a rock, I can see movement in the depths. One of the wiggling bodies turns up, as if drawn toward my presence, but it only gets near enough to the surface for me to see its arthropodan-shelled back and confirm it's a wraith, then the sunlight peaks over the canyon wall, a sharp ray glistening on the water.

The wraiths flee to the river's depths.

"Let's look downstream," I say. "Maybe some of our things got snagged along the bank."

Vaeryn spins around, pink swelled across her cheeks, and nods.

I take off my sopping boots and walk barefoot alongside the river. Neither of us speaks, our attention honed on our shaded surroundings. My body feels ten times tenser with the shadows draping the whole ravine and no bow at my back.

Stars, now what are we going to do?

16

EZRO

"THERE!" VAERYN CRIES AFTER A WHILE OF WALKING. I FOLLOW THE point of her finger to a gray mass wiggling on the river's edge.

I rush after it, recognizing it as her bag. Her arrows are still tucked in the attached quiver, and her bow is snug in its holster. *A miracle.* I fish it out and relief washes over her face as I hand it over. The bag's waxed surface drips, but when she inspects the inside, she smiles.

"The water barely got in," she says, fanning the dry pages of her journal. "With any luck, yours will be the same."

We walk a quarter mile downstream before I spot another lump in the water. I race to retrieve it, but as I close in, I can already see my luck isn't nearly as good. My bow is missing and at least half of my arrows, too. And worse, the heaviness of the bag suggests water got in.

Nerves tickle in my chest. *The Book of Illuminance—*

I tug my sopping blanket and clothes out. The heavy fabric flumps into the dirt. Drenched. I dump everything else out, excess water spilling across various tins and stuffed linen sacks. The last thing to fall is the book, now wrapped in a soaked shirt. *Why didn't I put it in something waterproof before getting on the river?*

I peel the clinging fabric away, exposing the wavy pages. Droplets slide across the leather cover, as I open it to where Mother signed it to me. The ink splotches over her words like watercolor, but it's still legible, at least. I sigh, gently lifting the soft page to check the damage to the book itself. Despite the water, the inscriptions are untouched. Mother *did* say it was blessed in many ways. Still, the pages will be warbled forever now.

I sprawl it on a rock to dry and begin wringing my spare clothes. They are just as wet as the ones I have on. I hang them in the trees, griping to myself all the while. My bow. Most of my arrows. Our boat. All gone. Everything else is soaked. *I'm* soaked.

I hate riverwraiths.

"The food is gone," Vaeryn says after a walk down the bank. "I found some of it floating loose down the river. There was nothing I could retrieve, but I found a few of your arrows."

I count five in her hand. Hardly anything, considering where we are. "No bow?"

She shakes her head with an apologetic smile.

I take the arrows and add them to the few in my quiver. She sits on a large rock, looking at her hands. Over her shoulder, I see blisters across her palms from pulling me out of the water. I sit on a rock across from her, my wet clothes sticking to my skin. I'd peel it all off if she wasn't here, but the thought of her seeing my bare skin—the scars Grandfather left on my back—is worse than the discomfort of drenched clothes. My spare clothes will dry soon enough, then I'll change.

"What do you want to do?" Vaeryn asks after a few minutes of stewing.

"What do you mean?"

Her gaze shifts between the trees. "Press on or turn back?"

For the first time since I talked her into letting me join her mission, I hesitate. Without food, we'll have to fish and forage to survive. Without the boat, we will have to travel on foot, which will be considerably slower. And now I don't even have a bow?

Turn back.

That's the only thing that makes sense. Stars, we'd be lucky to even survive the route home now. But my own words come back to haunt me. *I would do anything to see an Illuminarch return. Anything.*

"Press on," I say, though I could kick myself for it.

She doesn't even look my way. "We're not going to make it."

"We definitely won't if we don't try."

Vaeryn sits like a statue, absorbing my answer awhile before she nods and rises. She grabs her bow and holds it toward me. "Then you take this."

I stare at the pale wood, neither hand reaching for it.

"Take it." She shoves it closer. "It's better you have it than me. Put a mark on it. Take my arrows. Do the same. Of the two of us, only one can fight the netherbeasts, and it isn't me."

I grab it, watching the light douse in her eyes like she just handed me a piece of her soul.

"Thanks," I say, laying the bow on my lap. "And for coming after me, too."

She sits again, rubbing her blistered palms. "I can't fight them, but I promise not to be utterly useless otherwise. Your life is just as much my responsibility out here as mine is yours. But I will have to be more creative in how I defend it."

My gaze slides back to her hands. I sift through my scattered supplies, retrieving a jar. I open it and hold it out to her. "Aloe vera. So they don't get infected," I say when she hesitates.

She takes it and rubs the salve over her sores, wincing at the way it burns cold at the first touch. I dig into my bag again. "Got any linen wraps? Mine are soaked."

She looks at her greasy hands, then over to her bag. "Yes. Left pocket. If you don't mind."

It feels intrusive digging into her belongings, but she allowed it. I find the spool of bandage and carry it back to her. My first instinct is to pass it over and let her struggle through wrapping it around herself, but when our eyes meet, my mind changes.

"I'll do it," I say. "Hard to wrap your own hands."

She flinches like she might tell me to jump back in the river, but then her gaze drops to her feet, and she holds a hand toward me. I kneel, heart suddenly drumming in my chest. I support her wrist and the linen with one hand and start looping the light fabric to cover her palm with the other. With every circuit, my motions grow more rigid, more anxious, until I cut it loose with my knife and tuck it in.

Vaeryn looks up, her other hand still resting in her lap. For seconds that pass like an hour, I get lost in the details of her eyes. The way green speckles the blue, like sprouts trapped beneath ice—a promise of life growing behind her frigid exterior. But then she blinks, looks down so her eyelashes fan toward her red-splotched cheeks, and lifts her other hand.

I take it, feeling her gaze following my movements. I curse the hammering in my pulse. *Can she feel it? Where my thumb presses her wrist?*

Probably. Because I can feel hers too, and hers is doing the same. *Because she doesn't want me near her,* I remind myself.

I quickly finish and return the distance between us. Slowly, my pulse settles, but my hands take another ten minutes to forget what they just felt. Back in Rōsrun, when she'd grabbed my hand, all I'd felt was frustration. But this is something else. Something I've never been allowed to know.

Why is this happening?

The question rises with a spark of anger. I peel my focus from her and spend the next hour carving marks into her bow and all the arrows while she searches the area for food. After I've finished, I check on my spare clothes but find them still damp. I select the driest set and fan them to hurry the process along. I still need to sleep before nightfall.

When the clothes are dry enough, I gather them and walk upstream to change. I head back with every intention of going to sleep in the dirt since my blanket is still drenched, but when I return, Vaeryn has laid her blanket out with all my things set beside it. She motions to it and offers a smile signaling that it's for me, then turns before I can say anything and perches on a rock overlooking the river.

17

VAERYN

My sword pierces through the iridescent spine of a river trout. It wiggles a moment before the life drips from its unsuspecting body, and I add it to the others I've staked.

One more, I decide, stepping onto a smooth stone that protrudes from the gurgling water. My nerves surge with warning. Just because the riverwraiths already attacked once today doesn't mean they won't attack again. But what choice do I have? We must eat, and the land, at least as far as I'm willing to get from Ezro while he rests, has proven fruitless besides a fistful of pine nuts.

I survey the water with a firm grip on my sword. Thousands of tiny minnows dart under the crystalline surface. The trout favor the depths of the river, but graces know I'm not subjecting myself to the leap between here and the next stone. Patience, I trust, is all I need.

The afternoon sun watches me, slowly working a burn on my skin. But the stinging of its rays is mild compared to my palms. The aloe lessened the bite of my blisters for a time, but now blood has stained through the linen Ezro so delicately wrapped around them.

My lungs tense at the memory. The water still dripped off his hair from his near-drowning, and yet, he found the presence of mind to notice and tend to my minor injuries.

Graces. This is the last thing I need to dwell on.

I shirk off the memory just in time for a trout to make the mistake of approaching my blade. The gleaming tip sinks through it, and I hop back to land.

I gather the fish, careful not to let their juices drip onto my bandages and return to the fire I kindled after Ezro fell asleep. The flames dance steadily over the wood, billowing smoke that rises high above the spear-shaped trees before it diffuses into the blue. I leave the fish on a rock, deciding to seize Ezro's unconscious state and creep over to the book he left drying on a nearby rock.

My bare feet pad the ground in silent grace, but I check over my shoulder three times before I stop in front of it. Never once does he budge. Why would he care if I looked at it, anyway?

Or is it private? Like my journal?

Surely, he'd have said.

I lean, squinting at the open pages. On the left, a colorful painting of a man fills the space, framed with elegant whorls, much like the ones on his skin. He faces forward, eyes focused upward as if looking into the Elysium itself.

Illuminarch Bohan, I recognize, just before I see his name printed on the right side.

I fight a smile as my gaze returns to Ezro. *The Book of Illuminance.* How did he come to possess one of these? I thought my family had the last copies of it.

I crouch, seeing it harmless for me—the heiress—to be caught looking at it. Besides, the pages need to be flipped so it can dry better.

I delicately turn the water-logged pages until I find the most familiar face—my great-grandmother's. Though painted in the same pose as Bohan, something about her seems kinder than he. Perhaps it's the slight upturn of her lips, or the wideness of her eyes. But more likely, it's what Father taught me of her.

Though she'd died before he met her, Father heard stories from my grandfather of a ruler with a fiercely kind heart—one who would go to any length to protect her people. Clearly, as she died doing just that.

What would she think if she saw what happened after that?
If she looked at me?

"That's how I knew," Ezro says, right behind me.

I jolt, releasing a small shriek. "Graces, you're quiet. I thought you were still asleep."

He chuckles and kneels beside me, staring at the open page. "I noticed you looked familiar when you walked into the smithy, but I couldn't place it. Not until I looked at this again that night, right before I caught you playing tag with the necromancer."

"That's one way to say it."

He smiles, lifting the book off the rock. He holds it close to his face, pivoting between me and the illustration, and I wonder what he's thinking. Simply confirming the resemblance, or is he hoping I'll measure up to be half the Illuminarch she was?

"And just think, the next book will have you painted on the next page." He stares at Athenias a moment longer before he meets my gaze. "What an entry that will be. 'One hundred years after the massacre of Illuminarch Athenias and her Luminors, Vaeryn Seraphine rebirthed the lost order and redeemed the kingdom from the claws of the netherbeasts...'"

My lips flicker between a smile and frown. "I doubt my name will be the only one in here. The scribes will want to know *how* I managed to get that far."

He laughs, shutting the book. "Better get you that far first."

"How did you—" I say, just as he's shifting to stand, and he freezes. "How did you get one of these?"

He draws a long breath, turning his face toward the afternoon sky. "It was a gift from my mother. It was passed down from my grandfather, who'd managed to keep it hidden when the guards torched the others." The book hangs in his grip. "It's the only thing

I have of my mother's."

My shoulders lower at the solemn turn in his tone. "How old were you?"

"When she was taken? Almost twelve." His forehead crinkles, his gaze transfixed to the ground. The chatter of birds fills his long pause before he continues. "It was winter. Her favorite season because it's the only time the desert gets cool enough for a sweater. She'd just come home from her shift at the tavern and was changing into her nightclothes when I heard a pound at the door. I answered it, and our head Bronze Guard, Hena, pushed passed me, searching our house like a murderer was inside. When Mother came out, Hena snatched her. Asked if there were other traitors in the house. Mother shook her head—covering for me. Then Hena dragged her out without even letting us say goodbye."

I let his story seep in until my soul drinks it as if it's part of my own. "You were close with her?"

"When she was around. She worked a lot."

The warm breeze flutters a loose strand from my braid. I brush it behind my ear just as he's looking back, and his attention hones onto my red-stained hand wraps.

"Looks like you could use some fresh bandages," he says.

I bite my lip, not ready to move on from this conversation, but he walks toward our bags as if to tell me *he* is. I resign, unfurling the clinging linen from my hands, and follow him.

18

EZRO

My palm presses against a wall of wind-worn stone as we hike across a slim shelf on the cliff side. The river rushes at least fifty feet below, its full strength and depth forced between a tight narrowing in the canyon. I peak over the steep drop in vain hope that I'll spy the bow I lost yesterday stuck along the bank. The rolling currents glisten in the late afternoon light. The west wall will soon eclipse it, but from this height, the sun should protect us for at least another hour. Though, by Vaeryn's heat-splotched skin, I'm not sure I prefer the sunlight to the shadows.

I watch her slow footfalls closer than my own. The ground crunches under her boots and, occasionally, bits of dry earth crumble and rain down the steep slope on our right. The precariousness of it confuses me. Didn't the Luminors once use this portal to get in and out of the Etherium? How did they manage it without dying? And an even better question—

"Why is the portal to the Etherium in the canyon, anyway?"

"This place wasn't always ridden with monsters," Vaeryn says with a brief glance at me. Her face is redder than it was last time I saw it. "The journey to the portal was the means the Illuminant chose to select the first Illuminarch. You must not have read much of the histories in your book?"

"Like the pictures better," I tease. "My mother read the histories to me once, but I was so young. I don't really remember."

Vaeryn shakes her head, but I catch her subtle laugh.

"So, what's the story?"

"*Well*," she starts, an unfamiliar excitement filling her tone. "After Creation, the Illuminant knew he wanted to give someone charge over the people—a leader. But, of course, he wanted one whose heart was right and faith, strong." She pauses to catch her breath, but her words grow thinner the longer she speaks. "It's said the Illuminant spoke to the hearts of several men and women, prompting them to seek him in the canyon. Naturally, many of them either missed the call on their hearts or rejected it for the danger of voyaging into this uncharted place. The one with the faith to follow it was provided a guide, Raphós, who led him to the Etherium. He was then made the first Illuminarch. That man just happened to be my ancestor."

A limestone-stained breeze cools the sweat on my neck as I vaguely recall hearing some of this. "So what, did the Luminors have to travel through this canyon every time they wanted to go to the Etherium?"

"No. Father said there are portals leading to every major city, but an Illuminarch must activate them from inside the Etherium. Then, any of the Luminors could use them at will for the duration of that Illuminarch's life. But when an Illuminarch dies, the city portals seal."

"But this one doesn't?"

She glances back to smile at me, forehead sparkling with sweat. "Quite the opposite. It reopens when the Illuminarch dies, so that the next can find it and be anointed. The canyon is like a...rite of passage."

"Doesn't Solalé know about it? What's stopping her from going into the Etherium and messing with the Light?"

She pulls her hood overhead, so the shadow protects the top half of her face. "The Etherium is a holy place. Nothing of the netherworld can enter it."

"And there's no Bronze Guards protecting it, either?"

My question hangs awhile, the silence filled in by her labored breathing.

"She has the beasts," she finally answers, but her voice sounds hollow.

Her state quiets the rest of my questions so she can focus on keeping air in her lungs and minding her steps. My thoughts wander back to the tale of the first Illuminarch. What must that have been like? Traveling through this canyon, following a spirit with no understanding of why besides that the Illuminant said to? Did he have any idea what it would lead to?

And where is the spirit who led him now? For all Vaeryn has talked of him, I've yet to see him. Might he appear to lead us at some point? And will he help me defeat the netherbeasts guarding the portal?

A skid dissolves my musings, and my eyes refocus on Vaeryn. Her steps have gotten sloppier while my thoughts distracted me. She leans against the wall as she walks, feet barely rising for each step. Her toes butt a raised rock, and she stumbles. I reach toward her, but she turns for the wall, catching herself with her bandaged hands. Her eyes flutter, sweat shining on her unusually pallid face. Every breath she draws sounds weighted and forced.

"We should rest," I say.

She lets my words burn off in the blistering sun before shaking her head and turning onward.

I follow close behind. "Seriously, Vaeryn. You're not used to heat like this."

"We're almost to the shade," she says, her voice dry as the wind. "We'll rest there."

I look down the shelf. Not far ahead, it tapers into shadow. *Just a few more minutes. She'll make it.*

I hope.

"Let me carry your bag at least," I say.

She drags herself another two steps before reaching for the straps of her bag. She peels them off one at a time and turns. I reach for the bag, but before my fingers graze it, it flunks to our feet. Then suddenly, she's tipping. I lunge forward, hooking my arms beneath hers, and her limp body flops against my chest, staggering me a step back. Dirt crumbles beneath my heel on the edge of the shelf, and I lurch away as a clump of earth rains down the steep slope. My arms crush around Vaeryn as if the entire shelf was about to fall, but when the ground remains beneath my feet, my focus turns to the woman hanging as if dead in my arms.

Her hair tickles my chin. She's so close I can feel her every breath. I look at the path ahead and back to her. *What am I supposed to do? Carry her?*

My jaw clenches, realizing I have little choice. She'll die if I don't get her out of the sun.

Feet braced, I swing her so she's cradled in my arms. I press her tight against my chest and shimmy past her backpack, not wanting to risk bending for it while holding her. The stretch to the shade didn't look long a second ago. Now it looks as far away as the river.

I start ahead, feeling the burden of her dead weight with every step. This wouldn't be so hard if she could at least hold on. But then again, maybe that would be worse. Then she'd be conscious, fully aware of whose arms she's straddled in. Looking at me.

What would she think?

I'm answered by the memory of her wiping her hand off after holding mine back in Rōsrun. Twice, she wiped it. *She'd probably jump straight into the river.*

I glance at her every few steps to see if she's waking, but inside I'm pleading she'll wait until I've laid her down. She'd still figure out I carried her, but at least then it would already be over, and she wouldn't feel my strength shaking in my arms.

My nostrils are flaring by the time I reach the shadows. I all but crumple to the ground and lay Vaeryn down with what feels like the last of my energy. Her eyes are still shut. I must have gone faster than I realized—

Or her damage is worse than I thought.

She should be waking.

My heart stutters, but I keep moving. I wrestle her canteen from her belt but hear no sloshing. I shake it. Silence. I twist off the cap and look in. Dry.

Why didn't she tell me?

I grab my canteen instead, teetering it to gauge how much water is left by the splashing inside. *A quarter.* I sigh and peel my backpack off, fresh air brushing the back of my sweat-soaked shirt. It cools me by a petty degree. I dig out a couple of cloths from inside and soak them with what remains of my water. I lay one across her collarbone and use the other to dab water along her splotchy cheeks. My pulse drums in my ears just like it did while wrapping her hands yesterday. *How did I go from hammering steel to this?*

For a second, my motions unintentionally still, and I forget what I'm doing. Looking at her this closely, I notice things I didn't before. She has two little freckles dotted below her left eye, and that scar on her lip isn't the only one. There's another hidden in her hairline. I remember the cloth and pat it a few more times. All the while, imagining her waking, seeing me here and smiling in relief.

I almost laugh at myself. She'd be more likely to kick me in the gut and knock me off the cliff side.

I lay the cloth across her forehead, putting distance between us again, and force myself to concentrate. From deep in my memory, I unearth my mother's commands, ones she'd issued to me several times when dehydrated drunks in the tavern toppled in the Jarden heat. *Get her feet up,* I hear Mother say. I pull my backpack closer and lift Vaeryn's legs, so they rest on top of the bag.

Loosen her clothes.

My hands curl. *Sure, Mother, if I want to get shanked. Why aren't you here right now?*

But Vaeryn is strapped in armor—armor that is undoubtedly trapping heat against her.

If you want her to live…

I scowl and reach for the least offensive place I can—an armguard—but just before I grab one, Vaeryn's eyes open. I recoil my hand, hiding the evidence of what I was about to do—even if for good reason. She stares at me, eyelashes fluttering, before she looks around in several jerky motions.

"You fainted," I say.

She squints at me, then down the shelf where her abandoned bag sits and back to me. Her lips part like she wants to speak, but then her eyes threaten to shut her away again.

"We're out of water. I need to go down to the river," I say, and her eyes open wider. "You need to get your armor off."

She stares again, as if she's seeing two of me.

"It's trapping the heat," I explain. "Can you do it?"

Another long stare, then finally she nods.

"Okay. I'll be right back," I say, but the exhausted way she's looking at me keeps me from standing. It pulls me back to a time when Niah was ill with a fever that wouldn't relent for anything. Every time I tended to her, she'd give me that same look. *Empty*, like she was too weary to even notice who was there. And I feel the same fear I did then.

What if I don't do enough? What if those eyes turn cold right in front of me?

"You're going to be okay," I say to her because it makes me think it's true. She gives me a weak smile—more than Niah ever managed.

I detach my quiver and bow from my backpack to wear them without the added weight, and with one last glance at her, I dash down the shelf, hoping to find a place to downclimb before Vaeryn is completely out of sight.

19

VAERYN

Consciousness ebbs like the tide as I wait in shadows with no armor and no means of defending myself. But in my exhaustion, I can't muster the strength to worry. Instead, I fade in and out of a memory of a time not terribly different from now.

A week into setting out with Verik, I'd fallen ill, but the fear of asking him to slow down kept me quiet about it. He was so eager to reach the Etherium and so resolved that *haste* was our greatest defense against the dangers that I treaded through the late spring snow, burning with a fever. I muffled my coughs, but I know he still heard them.

He never said anything.

I forced myself on until the weakness from the fever overtook me, and I collapsed into the snow. It took at least twenty paces before Verik even noticed I was down.

He whipped around, skin creased between his brows. "What's the matter?"

I stared at him, wondering how he couldn't tell. I never took him for a fool, but his determination seemed to have blinded him.

"I need to rest, Verik. I have a fever," I said.

His head cocked to the side, anger flashing in his eyes before he pressed a smile back on. *Ah, the mark. He's fighting it again.*

"Ryn, it's *day*," he said, his tone like a rose prickled with thorns. "We need to keep going while the sunlight protects us. There's a town a few miles from here. Can you not make it?"

I clutched the snow, squeezing it between my palms. It melted against my warmth. My mind churned for a proper answer. Something that might bring my Verik back fully, without the nether-magic-spurred anger brimming under his skin.

"Perhaps if you carry me," I teased with a smile he once said he could never say no to.

His laugh blistered the air. "Carry you? Don't tell me the future Illuminarch can't handle a little fever." His steps trampled the snow between us, and he reached out his hand.

Hesitantly, I took it, just to be jerked to my feet so hard I felt a near rip in my socket.

He smiled again, a charming, innocent type of smile. "You can do this, Ryn."

I stood on shaking knees. The fever burned all the way into my eyes, and I felt the tears welling in them. *What's wrong with me? The entire kingdom is counting on me, and I'm whining over a fever.*

I nodded to him, pained yet grateful that he pushed me on, because in the moment, it felt like he was right.

But all this time later, it doesn't feel right anymore. The next town was three miles out. I could have died just to spare us a delay.

But you didn't. I hear Verik's voice in my head. *I got you to safety. And where are you now? Safe?*

I look around again, eyes slowing over my shed armor. *No, I'm more vulnerable than I've ever been.*

I try to sit, but flecks of light crowd my vision and force me down. I shut my eyes, just succumbing to my weakness when I hear steps. I jolt toward them, fearing a netherbeast has found me here in the shade, but I spot Ezro jogging across the shelf. Waves of blackness sweep over me. Every time I clear them, he's a little closer until he's crouching beside me.

"Here. Can you sit up?" he says, holding my filled canteen toward me with one hand and offering me aid with the other. I accept it, letting him pull me upright. Another surge of sparks surrounds my vision, but I suddenly fear it less.

He opens the canteen and presses it into my hand. I bring it to my lips, sipping it at first, and eventually gulping it down. The water runs through me like cool rain sinking through a parched land. Ezro grabs one of the cloths I'd laid aside when they became too hot and soaks it fresh with his own water. He hands it to me when I'm finished drinking, and I hold it to my face.

"Just give me a few minutes," I say. "Then we can press on. I don't want to waste the light."

"The light will come back tomorrow," Ezro says.

My arm weakens, lowering the cloth from my face. I meet his gaze. The way he watches me is like he expects me to drop dead any moment. So...

Worried.

Verik didn't look like that. In fact, if anything, he seemed irritated by my condition. Of course, when I'd confronted him, he said the same thing he always did.

"I'm so sorry, Ryn. It's this mark. It's making me not myself."

"I wish you'd never gotten it," I'd said.

His next words had come out like ointment on a wound. "I had to. For you. Everything I do is for you."

Ezro suddenly stands, his motion diffusing my memories. I watch him run back for my bag. When he returns, he drops it beside me, and I catch a fleeting glimpse of the crescent stained on his wrist. Strange, he's had it so long, and yet, I've never once seen it control him.

"Does time make it easier?" I ask.

He sits across from me. "As long as you stay in the shade. I'd say go cool off in the river, but it's too fast. Steep climb down, too."

"Not that." I sip my water to regain more of my voice. "The mark. It never seems to bother you. I always heard it gets harder to resist its temptations the longer you have it."

He looks at the crescent. "Nothing can have power over you unless you let it. Just have to train yourself to resist it."

My thumb taps the side of my canteen. "And how do *you* resist it?"

He stares at me a while before his chin lowers, his hair hanging over his face. "My mother left me a note in that book. 'Never change.' I mean to heed that, even if she's not around to see it."

"Is it really that simple?"

"On the surface."

"Then what's beneath it?"

His head snaps upright, hair flipping from his eyes. He smiles. "Odd topic to be thinking about right now."

"Well?"

"Guess I'm just used to restraining myself," he says, the smile washing from his face. "Holding my tongue. Clenching my fists. Been doing that since I was born. Being at Grandfather's..." He looks down at the river like he wished it would carry his memories away. "Learned it for good there. The mark is no different. I've learned to ignore it as well as anything. And doing it for my mother; that makes it easier."

I seal my lips, absorbing his response. *What is it then? Has Ezro's broken life just made him that much stronger than Verik? Or was Verik just using the mark as an excuse?*

No, the hold it had on him was real. No one could be the gentle man I knew in Brïsbrook only to lash out in such ways.

Could they?

I press the thoughts down like a bubble underwater, bound to resurface, and latch my focus on what Ezro said. "Perhaps that's why the Illuminant allowed it all. To make you resilient. He didn't want you to succumb to the mark."

His jaw clenches so tight I see it dimple. "*Worked.*"

I frown, wanting to ask for more details about what happened. But sensing it's an unwelcome question, I propose a change of topic. "I don't feel sore. You must have caught me."

He fixes on his usual smirk. "You flopped against me like a dead fish. Didn't have much of a choice."

"And you *carried* me over here?"

He nods. "You're heavy for such a small person."

I swallow, the scene playing in my mind but not by memory. A familiar flutter scurries through my chest, and now I wish I didn't mention it at all. Except that some selfish part of me wanted to know how he felt about it and to confirm what I believed happened.

Yet Verik laughed at the notion of carrying me.

"You could have dragged me," I say when I notice the silence.

"Seemed indecent," he says. "Besides, I paid a lot for those clothes. Wouldn't want them getting torn up."

We both chuckle. The sound is short and quiet, but it resettles my nerves. *What I would have given to have a friend like this all those months I traveled alone.*

"Really, I think we can press on," I say. "I'm all right now."

He studies me as if evaluating the shade of my face to gauge how "all right" I truly am. Then he stands, snatching both of our bags before I can even reach for mine.

"You feel even a little off, tell me," he says.

"I will."

20

EZRO

By nightfall, we're back at the base of the canyon, a quarter mile from the river. A dip in the water and the cooler ravine air returned Vaeryn to her full strength and stubbornness. Now she's wandering alone, scavenging, while I set up camp. I listen to the monstrous ruckus that fills the canyon every night, waiting for her scream to pierce through it. The longer it doesn't come, the more I expect it. If she'd just waited a few minutes so we could go together, she'd have spared me a heap of stress, but after her faint on the cliff, she seems twice as determined to prove she can hold her own.

Except she *can't*. It doesn't matter how fast or skilled she is if her weapons pass through netherbeasts like fog.

I lay the kindling and light it. The flames wriggle across the juniper branches, inciting a pungent, fruity aroma into the air. I scan the obscure surroundings again for Vaeryn, but all I find are tree trunks glowing in the fire's light and a vast spread of grass-splotched dirt. My fingers twitch. *Maybe I should go look for her.*

I turn the way she went, but don't step. Seeking her out would further crumble her pride, and after all, what else does she have to hold on to?

I shake my head, laughing at this odd woman I've found myself out here with. I unfurl her blanket a short stretch from the fire and spread it until every corner is perfectly distributed.

I turn for mine when, *finally*, I hear footsteps crunching back to camp. My eyes lift to the star-flecked sky in a silent "thank you" to the Illuminant, then I turn to chide Vaeryn for taking so long.

But the words catch in my throat at the sight of an antlered figure draped in tattered robes standing in her place.

The necromancer.

The muzzle of his deer skull face points straight for me, hollow eyes seeming to move in the flickering firelight. His boney hand thumps his feathered staff against the ground, once. Twice. The third time, wind swirls the dirt at his feet.

The bronze crescent tingles on my wrist. I retrieve my bow and aim an arrow for where I should have put it the first time I'd seen him. Straight in his eye socket.

The arrow flies and sinks seamlessly into its target.

But the necromancer doesn't drop. Instead, he jerks his head to the side, and the arrow falls out, worthless. It hits the whirling ground where feet are materializing from the dust and wind. *Human* feet, dressed in familiar boots.

My heart stops.

Vaeryn?

I watch the legs forming, petrified to do anything. *I've failed her. She's dead—*

The spectral body reaches the hips, and I realize I don't recognize these clothes. It's not what Vaeryn had on, and this ghost seems too tall. The relief spurs me into motion. I trade my bow for my staff, twisting the sides together as three more spirits emerge in the wind and dust—a legion of befallen bandits.

The bandits from Dunas, I realize as they draw their weapons.

I raise my staff just in time to block the broadsword of the swiftest opponent. An unnatural metal whir vibrates in my ears, like the howls of the coyotes—everywhere and nowhere. Its dizzying resonance tosses my focus, and I miss the next offending strike. The sword rakes against my steel breastplate. I stagger back into a merciless entourage of blades. My staff spins into action like a windmill caught in a hurricane. The unearthly clang of steel-on-steel bounces off the canyon walls in a warlike commotion.

Between my wild swings and jabs, I glance at the necromancer. He's walking away—in the same direction Vaeryn ventured in.

She's still out there.

A sharp cut across my shoulder pulls my full attention back to the madness I'm locked in. Another sword pierces through my defense, splicing the leather side of my armor. The blade reaches my skin; just a scratch. The burn is petty compared to my shoulder.

I bash my staff against another sword and risk another glance toward the necromancer. All I catch is the pointed end of his antlers before he disappears into the shadows.

A blade swipes into my peripherals, and I finally get a clean enough blow to knock the sword from the offender's phantom hand. He turns for his weapon, and I deliver what would be a skull-splitting bash to his head if he were flesh. The spirit dissolves, but the other three respond in an instantaneous assault. I roll my staff, battering the blades, but one still breaks through and adds another slice to my arm.

My temples thrum. The longer I take to get through these spectral bandits, the more likely it gets that the necromancer will find Vaeryn. And then what? He kills her and sends her spirit to finish me off?

She probably could.

I sidestep another swipe and, with a spin, bash the aggressor like I did the first. Another shower of dust rains from where he stood, leaving me with two bandit souls to liberate from the necromancer's ownership.

But the remaining two prove themselves far more agile than the first. They dodge and bar my assaults with skill level with my trainer,

Sterling, himself. Except I never had to fight *two* Sterlings. My staff clangs against the blades so often it sounds like Grandfather and I both hammering at our anvils. But here, between every metallic clank, is my pounding breath and grating soles as I skid and slide and swerve.

But then, I hear it. The sound I was so expectant for earlier.

Vaeryn's scream—in the form of my name.

The sound pierces my core. *My name. Called.*

And I can't answer it.

Heat ruptures under my skin, and my every motion heightens. In seconds, another assailant dissolves beneath my blow, leaving me with only one bandit left—the swordswoman the necromancer conjured first.

I dip beneath her blade and rise with a strike to her core. It stammers her backward, but her sword remains cleaved. She grunts, the sound more animalistic than human, and slashes after my throat. I parry it, then feint toward her knees. She falls for it, and I turn my staff sideways, pushing her to the ground. I sneak my knife out and finish the ghost off with a swipe across her throat.

I rise as she disintegrates, batting my eyes to clear the images of the spectral, yet human, faces I just *fully* killed. An act of mercy is what it really is. I released them to their proper fate, yet I can't help feeling like a murderer.

But I don't have time to hate myself for it, not when Vaeryn's gone silent. Where is she? Alive? Dead?

Is her soul the next one I'll have to release?

I dash down the ravine, wounds stinging across my arms. The firelight fades into blackness before I finally spot the silhouette of the necromancer. His staff points toward the ground, where Vaeryn writhes and groans, strangled in roots from her feet to her throat.

I charge after the necromancer, but he turns, conjuring another whirlwind with a single beat of his staff. From it, a mountain lion emerges with a raucous snarl. It pounces toward me, jaw wide and ready to tear the skin from my face. I thrust my staff horizontally, catching it behind the teeth, but its weight and velocity throw me onto my back, and I lose it. I roll, narrowly dodging a sharp swipe to the head, and scurry to my feet. Vaeryn whines, the noise even more constrained than when I first arrived.

My heart pounds like a war drum. *She's running out of air.*

I wallop the mountain lion's shoulder, hard enough to cripple. It roars for the whole canyon to hear and rears up, pointed teeth ready to sink into my flesh. I slide my foot back, preparing my balance this time, and catch it like I did before. My staff hinges behind its teeth like a horse's bridle, and I crank it to the right, snapping its neck. Dust coats my boots.

I fill my lungs and charge after the necromancer while his attention is still fixated on squeezing the last of Vaeryn's oxygen from her. I raise my staff, readying to swing it straight into his deer skull head.

But instead, it collides with his staff. The wood cracks, but doesn't break. Then he points it at something behind me and swings. I turn just quick enough to duck beneath the rock hurtling toward me, only for another to hit me on the opposite side, jerking the air from my lungs. The necromancer aims and tosses another—this one large enough to crack my skull. I evade it by a hair's breadth, feeling its wind as it passes me by.

But just as he's lifting a boulder that could crush me, Vaeryn yelps my name again. The boulder drops, the necromancer unable to command both the roots and rocks at once. He twists to tighten her bounds, and I seize his fleeting distraction with a race forward. My staff swings. He turns—

But his defense isn't quick enough.

Metal rams against bone, and his head flings nearly to the river. It cracks against a stone and the rest of his skeleton clatters to my feet, his dirty clothes slumping over it.

Vaeryn gasps, and I rush to her side, knife snapping through the roots tangled around her. I slice at them until she's free, my hands shaking with adrenaline.

"Are you okay?" I ask.

But her bloodshot eyes fix in the distance, and I register the rattling sound behind me. I look back and see the pile of bones shaking, pieces rejoining. Across the way, the cracked skull skids an inch over, as if pulled by a string toward the rest of his body.

"The staff," Vaeryn whispers. "Break the staff."

I leap up, racing for the staff as the necromancer's knees reconnect.

Vaeryn shouts at me just before I grasp it, "Ezro, wait!"

But I don't process her words quick enough, and I'm holding the staff before I can ask what she means. The necromancer's bones jangle apart and go still at my feet, but the staff burns cold against my palm, like a shaft of ice. My nails dig into the crack I put in the wood. One good hit against a rock is all it should take, and yet—

My body doesn't move.

The cold crawls across my skin, a sudden wind whooshing around me.

Its gusts fill with the necromancer's hissing whispers.

Claim it, he says. *Wield it. Use it against Solalé.*

My grip tightens on the staff, a shadow creeping over my very soul.

You could raise an army from the beasts in this canyon. Take them to the capital and unleash them on your enemies.

I inhale, and the air tastes like iron. The cold deepens through the layers of my skin, sharpest where my mark is. And I can hear it. The nethermagic stained on me screaming to connect with this instrument of power. To do as the necromancer says.

My mind fills with flashes of how it would play out. I'd spend the next week or two no longer running from but *hunting* the netherbeasts. I'd slaughter them, beast after beast, and with their slain souls, I could storm the capital, sic them on the Bronze Guards, on *Solalé*, and—

Claim the kingdom for yourself, hisses the necromancer.

The sound of people cheering—for me—fills my ears. Among them, I hear voices I know. *Father. Grandfather. Niah.* Their acceptance turns my vision dark with need. My family. *Wanting me.*

But through the commotion, another voice calls my name. *Mother.* And just as suddenly as one notices a spider crawling up their leg, I realize what's happening. What the necromancer is doing. Tempting me. Playing on my weakness. My desperation to be seen.

My mind snaps clear, and I feel the ground firm beneath my feet again.

"Go back to the netherworld," I say into the wind.

I swivel toward the first tree I see and smash the staff against it. The wood cracks in half, splinters flying, and the wind ceases like a door shutting out a storm.

21

EZRO

I toss the broken pieces of the necromancer's staff into our campfire, and the flames begin gnawing them to ash. I sit to watch, pulse still thrumming in my ears. Across the fire, Vaeryn stares at me like she doesn't notice I'm looking. Her eyes are as wide as they were when I defeated the necromancer, and only the slightest curve of her lips suggests it's not terror keeping her that way, but something else. Surprise, maybe. As if she never expected I could really do it—could really conquer a netherbeast—when we first agreed to do this together.

She wouldn't be the only one surprised.

A sting in my shoulder reminds me of the new stripes I earned in the first wave of battle. I tug at my sleeve, looking through the slit to inspect the damage, but I can hardly see it around the curve of my shoulder. Down my arms, I find a few little nicks. Nothing worth whining over. Grandfather's done worse. Still, they'll need tending.

"You still have my aloe?" I ask Vaeryn, only to see she's already digging for it.

She retrieves the jar and a couple of cloths from her bag and holds them, biting the edge of her lip like she's considering something. But whatever it is seems to pass, and she hands everything over, hardly meeting my eyes despite all her previous staring.

I peel my torn outer shirt off and wet one of the cloths to wipe my arms clean. Blood dyes the white towel red. I smear aloe onto my lesser cuts, then twist to examine the wound on my shoulder. From what little I can see, I can tell it needs stitching, but *how* I'm supposed to reach back there to do it—

Vaeryn suddenly sits beside me, and, with no warning, she lays her hand against my bare shoulder and inspects the laceration herself. "I'm not very good at stitching," she says, returning to her bag. "But I suppose I'll have to do."

"You don't have to—"

She shoots me a look, digs a needle and spool from her bag, and returns to my side. "You saved my life…*again*…the least I can do is sew up the damage you earned in doing so. You aren't afraid of a little needle, are you?"

"Just not used to being helped."

She searches my eyes like she's sifting through their memories to validate what I said. Then she blinks out of it and pulls the cloth from my hand.

"Well, I can't promise I'll be a great help, but I certainly will try," she says, patting the wound clean.

I try not to watch her as she threads the needle or to notice that, despite her sturdy expression, her fingers shake. But that's all I can see until the needle sinks into my skin.

Twenty minutes later, Vaeryn retracts her hand with a grimace toward her handiwork. I can see only an inch of her stitches, and while it's admittedly sloppy, it's better than what I could do on my own.

She cleans the needle and her hands, but just when I'm expecting her to put distance between us again, she meets my eyes. "I don't know how you did that," she says.

"What?"

"Resisted him even with that mark."

My head tilts toward the sky where a sliver of a crescent like the one on my wrist hangs between the lofty canyon walls. "Guess faith is stronger."

Vaeryn smiles, going quiet for a while before meeting my gaze again. "Can I ask you something?"

"You're the Illuminarch," I say, barely remembering to add levity to my tone. "You can ask whatever you want, and I'd have to answer."

She rolls her eyes. "Not yet, and even once I am, I don't think such rules should apply to friends."

Friends. The word lays across me like a coat in the cold. *When was the last time I had one of those?*

"Thought I was just your bodyguard."

"*Please*," she says. "You've been a friend to me since I walked into that smithy."

My smile spreads. "Well, what's your question?"

"What would you be doing right now if the kingdom was already as it should be?"

My forehead wrinkles. *Random.*

"You mean if there was already an Illuminarch on the throne?"

"Yes. Say, Solalé and the witchlord never came. What life would you choose?"

My inhale stretches my lungs, and I have to mull my answer over several moments before I finally shake my head. "No idea, Vaeryn. That would mean my grandfather and father weren't marked. That they never gave into the corruption. I have no idea who I'd be if they were different. What I'd be doing."

She soaks in my answer, another question rising in her eyes, but I shoot mine faster.

"What about you? Your father would probably be on the throne then, right? How would you be spending your royal days?"

She rubs her throat where the roots burned into her skin. "Honestly, I'm not sure either. Who am I if not this?"

"I hope you find out someday," I say. "I'll do whatever it takes to make sure you get the chance."

Her shoulders relax, then she stands with a soft chuckle to herself. "The world needs more people like you."

"What, desperate and under-slept?"

She snorts. "No. I mean…" Her eyes scan the canyon walls as if the words she's looking for might be etched up there.

"Oh, you mean bullheaded perfectionists?"

"*Closer.*" She laughs, and I shut my mouth long enough for her to deliver her answer. "I mean people who don't perpetuate pain with pain, but rather alchemize it into determination and bravery to do good."

"Would have never guessed that," I joke, despite the goosebumps on my arms. "Is that what's really in your records? Poetry?"

"Maybe a little." She returns to her side of the fire, her smile unfading.

Looking at her, my chest loosens like prison bars opening after six years of being sealed shut. And for this one night, I forget who she's to become. Who I am. Where we are. All I see is that for the first time in years, I have a friend. And now I'm certain I'll die in this place to keep her safe if it comes to it.

22
EZRO

A hand jostles my shoulder, and I startle awake, eyes opening to Vaeryn's ashen face just inches from mine.

"Something's here," she whispers.

I snatch my bow and rise, exhaustion falling off me like a blanket. My fresh wounds from last night burn as I skim the mosaic of shadows spattered around us and back to Vaeryn. She points to her ear. *Listen.* I still my breath, tuning my attention to every slight noise in the canyon. The shushing of the river. The far-out cry of a falcon. The gentle scratching of leaves in the breeze.

I shake my head, and Vaeryn holds a finger out, squinting like she expects to hear it again at any moment. But seconds pass, then a minute, and her hand lowers to her side again.

"I swear I heard something," she mutters.

"What did it sound like?"

"Like something heavy dragging across the ground."

I wait another minute and when nothing comes of it, I say, "Let's hope whatever was doing the dragging is satisfied with what it found." I crouch to stuff my things into my bag. "We should get away from here."

Vaeryn agrees with a curt nod and gathers her belongings.

In sync, we sling on our bags and stride for the river. We walk along its edge, lips sealed, and ears perked for the sound. But all I notice is the quiet deepening the higher the sun gets. Its light hems the east wall now, a splash touching the top of the west wall. It seems like this is what most of my days are consumed by now—watching the light enter and leave the ravine, waxing and waning my state of vigilance with it. But something about the necromancer finding us last night has cranked my anxiety into full gear, as if he was the barrier between the luck we've had and the *real* way things should be going out here. And while defeating him boosted my confidence, I have a crippling feeling it will shatter the moment I see the size of the true monsters in this canyon.

Will I be enough?

That's the question I've been asking myself all my life, but it's never meant as much as it does now. The fate of the entire kingdom rests in Vaeryn's hands, and her fate rests in mine. Which really means that, right now, it's all up to me.

The sun slowly spreads into the base of the canyon. My tension releases, and I stuff my bow away. I only get a few hours of this—the sense of safety—before darkness trickles back in. But at least now we have an opportunity to get ourselves far away from whatever Vaeryn heard.

I glance at her. Normally, I'd take the sunlight as my cue to start a conversation, but despite the protection radiating all around us, she still looks as stressed as she did when I woke. *What went on in her head while I was sleeping?*

Her thumb rubs her teardrop pendant, a faraway look in her eyes saying she's lost somewhere miles away from me in her mind. *Somewhere with Verik.*

I fix my eyes ahead, trying to focus on the path, but the longer I leave the silence, the more she stings my peripheral vision.

What if she's wishing I was him right now?

"Tell me about him," I say.

Her hand drops like it does every time she realizes I've caught her messing with her pendant. "What more is there to tell?"

"I don't know. What was he like?"

Her lips twist to the side. "Why? What interest is it of yours who he was?"

"Just thought maybe you might want to talk about it. Someone died and your journal's the only one you've told about him. Seems wrong."

She sighs, leaving me to listen to our footsteps for the longest time. Then finally she clears her throat. "In many ways, like you. But in others, quite the opposite."

"How?"

She side-eyes me. "Well, you share his stubborn nature. His wit. Bravery."

"What's different?"

"You're tan," she says with a smirk.

"Not if we stay in this ravine much longer."

She laughs, but it sounds distant, like she's down in a pit. One she doesn't even try to climb out of. Almost as if she thinks it's where she belongs.

"He also favored long-winded ways of saying things," she adds. "While it's hard to get more than a sentence from you at a time. If that."

"So, he liked to listen to himself talk?" I tease.

"One might say." Her smile fades like a slow-falling sunset. "But he was good at it. The way he told stories, anyone would listen for all the length it took for him to tell them."

The fondness in her tone sours my tongue. There's no competing with someone who's dead—especially not when they died the way he did. *For her.* And while I'd just as soon do the same, the look in her eyes suggests there's no place left in her heart for anything more than what she called me last night. A friend. Not that it would matter, anyway. She's about to become the Illuminarch. I have no place expecting more than friendship, if even that lasts after her anointing.

"There are more ways you two are different." Her gaze lowers along with her tone. "He wasn't nearly as resistant to the mark as you. In fact, I fear that had he been left to break the necromancer's staff, he'd have not done it. Watching you last night..." Her lips twitch like she's searching for the right way to say it, but then her feet stop, and she faces me. "I just don't understand how it works. How could you have the mark so long and yet be so unaffected? And yet, Verik, he..."

The unusual fear swimming in her tone lowers my brows.

"What did he do?" I ask.

She turns as if he were right beside her, saying her name. Her lips turn pale, and she leaves me waiting far too long.

"He just...changed," she starts, the vibrance doused from her voice. "He was one man in Brïsbrook, and fifty miles out, another."

"What do you mean?"

She strokes her forehead. "Well, if you knew him in Brïsbrook, you'd know him as someone everyone wanted to be around. Funny, smart. Full of interesting ideas and experiences. And he was kind then. Always noticing the smallest shifts in me. *Graces*, I swear that man could sense I was having a bad day from across town." She looks ahead like she means to start walking again but doesn't move. "I suppose that's why it was so alarming when, after we set out alone, he started behaving differently. As if there were two different people living inside of him. One, the man I knew, and another, a stranger.

"This other version of him was impatient, harsh even, and utterly obsessed with reaching the Etherium as quickly as possible. All his jokes became barbed. His stories, once humbly told, became self-glorifying. 'Look what I did, look what I'm doing now.' That's all he seemed to be saying." Her posture sags. "But then the Verik I knew would come back. Gentle, caring. Willing to do anything for me. He teetered between them so often, he could shift from one man to the next in a single conversation. It was...confusing, but, of course, he chalked it up to the mark. He said it was making him behave that way, and since he got it on my behalf, there was nothing I could do but blame myself, too."

I stare at her with my jaw clenched, trying not to show that, inside, I'm blazing. All this time, she's talked about him like he's the greatest man to breathe air, and now this?

How dare he.

How dare he turn his inability to resist the mark on her. How dare he strangle her in guilt like that, so tight that even in his death she's still choking.

And how could it happen so suddenly? Or did he just give up pretending he was someone else as soon as he had her dependent on him?

"I'm sorry… I shouldn't have…" Vaeryn shifts away.

I almost reach for her, nearly overcome with a need to bring her close to me, but I let my hand droop back to my side. No matter who Verik became, she's still in love with the version of him she once knew. But which side of him was real?

"Don't apologize," I say. "I'm the one who asked."

She glances at me, her nose ruddy. "It's wrong to speak ill of the dead."

"Telling someone the truth about them is not speaking ill." I fight another urge to step closer to her. "Even if the truth is ugly."

"I feel like I ruined him," she says as if I'd said nothing. "I shouldn't have ever agreed to him joining the Bronze Guards to help me. Then he never would have changed. Never would have died…"

"None of that is your fault."

She whirls around, piercing me with her eyes. "How is it not my fault? He did it all for *me.*"

"You didn't *make* him."

She clutches the pendant. "He was *in love* with me."

"Was he?"

Her mouth falls ajar, and I wish I could suck the question back into my mouth.

"What's that supposed to mean?" she asks.

"You just told me he turned into someone else the moment you got away from home, then blamed you for it. That doesn't exactly sound like love to me," I say, choosing my words with the caution of a poet.

"It was *the mark.*"

Frustration bristles my skin. *Now she sounds like Mother defending Father.*

"Even if it was, he still let it have control," I say. "He still let it hurt you."

Her arms cross. "Even if it was?"

Stars, now what have I done?

My hands ball at my sides, but it's too late to back out now. I'm in the fight. I just hope she can see she's the one I'm fighting for.

"The nethermagic in this mark adds nothing new to anyone," I say, holding up the crescent. "It can only build on the darkness that's already inside us and increase the impulse to act on it. And the more you give in, the harder it is to resist it. But six years fighting it, and I can tell you one thing. The antidote—the most powerful resistance—is loving someone. Loving them more than yourself—that conquers the need to respond to those impulses. Because you'd rather die to yourself than see them hurt. So, I'm having a tough time believing that someone can claim to love you and yet so easily let the mark incite them to hurt you. And for him to blame you for his actions on top of it... That's not love, Vaeryn. That's called control. And believe me, I know all about it."

Her arms tighten over her chest, knuckles white for how hard she's holding herself. She stares at me like she's looking through a pane of glass and beyond it, her whole life is up in flames.

And I started the fire.

"That's just...the way it seems to me," I say, hoping it'll soften the blow of what I said, but she doesn't even blink at my words like she's gone deaf.

I feel the sweat rising on my neck. Any second, she's going to snap. Scream. Throw something. Tell me to get lost. Either that or I just broke her, sent her mind into an abyss she'll never return from.

Why couldn't I just keep my mouth shut?

Finally, she blinks and jerks her face away from me. "Illuminant, help me," she mutters, and rushes ahead like she means to leave me behind.

"I'm sorry," I say, rushing after her anyway.

She doesn't speak to me again until nightfall, and when she does, her voice is cold and impersonal, issuing a warning about the nether-beast she'd heard before. *Our scent will be easy to follow. Be extra vigilant.*

Then she's curled on her side, holding that pendant through every hour of my watch.

23
VAERYN

My ears buzz as I scribble in my journal beneath the vague morning light. Page after page, I fill the white space with the screams from my soul. The words are hardly legible, and the thoughts are a disastrous mess of memory, thoughts, and questions. I should have done this before attempting to sleep last night—then, perhaps, rest may have found me. Instead, I lay awake through the night, clenching a cry in my throat so Ezro wouldn't hear it.

I still couldn't speak to him when we traded shifts. Even looking at him makes me sick—which only makes me feel worse. It's not his fault, what he said. I keep telling myself that. All he did was offer me a person to grieve to. I'm the one who saw it as my opportunity to use him as a sounding board.

But perhaps I should have considered whether or not I was ready to confront reality, because now Ezro is the face of it. His voice—the one that spoke my fears straight into my ears.

That's not love, Vaeryn. That's called control.

I can't stop hearing him say it. Again and again, like hooves trampling over me.

And behind his voice, I hear my mother yelling at me after I first told her my intentions of taking on Father's quest with Verik at my side.

"He's using you, Vaeryn. He doesn't care about you! He wants the Light, and if you're the only way to it, he'll do whatever it takes to get it."

"How could you say that about him? He's a follower of the Illuminant!" I yelled back.

"He's a Bronze Guard."

"Only so he can help me!"

Red blistered across Mother's face. "I don't trust him."

"You don't trust anyone."

She calmed then, approaching me with a sickly tender look in her eyes. "Something just feels off to me about him. I'm worried about you, Vae, that's all. I don't want anything bad to happen to you. We're safe here…"

"I'm tired of safe," I snapped.

I walked away before she could say anything else, but now the guilt is twisting like a cyclone in my gut. What if she's right? Not only did I put the Light in danger with my arrogance, but I also hurt my mother in the process—my mother, who's spent her entire life trying to protect me. Her means have been questionable, and at times, infuriating, but there's no doubting her genuine love.

How could I dismiss her like that?

I flip to the next page of my journal, just dotting it with ink when an inclination comes over me. I set the pen aside and flip back to the beginning, reading over my earliest reflections. They are revolting at first. I took this journal, empty, from my father's study and committed its pages to the journey ahead. It begins with me recounting how I'd stolen Father's map the night before he'd planned to leave. I'd almost lost my nerve—suffocated by the responsibility succeeding at this mission would lead to. But Verik had encouraged me that final day that we could do it together and reminded me that my father was doomed on his own with his bad leg, and therefore, so was the kingdom if *I* didn't go.

I pass the next dozen pages. I don't want to read anything about the first few days of our traveling—the days when Verik was still himself. I land on a page that begins with, "I don't know what I did," and I begin skimming the rest of the journal from there. As I read, a film of tears slowly blurs my vision until I can barely see. So many of the pages are repeats of the same thing. Him having some form of outburst, me either shrinking right away or attempting to defend myself, only for him to switch back to his sweet self and apologetically remind me how he got that way. Over and over and over until I'm about to slam the book shut and start a fire to burn it.

But then I stumble on a page that slows me. It recounts a conversation, line by line, as best I could remember it.

"You look troubled," Verik said.

My soul melted. He was himself. Otherwise, he'd have not noticed.

"I'm just worried," I said. "Even if we make it to the Light, there's still so much more for me to do, and I can't help but fear the kingdom will reject the idea of an Illuminarch returning. They are so conditioned now to believe the Illuminant abandoned us. It seems an Illuminarch returning after all these years would induce frustration and distrust amongst the people... I'm not sure I am ready to bear this burden, Verik."

He sat quietly a long while, before his hand suddenly slipped into mine. My heart fluttered.

"Vaeryn, I know becoming the Illuminarch isn't really what you want. It's never been. It wasn't right for Liander to reject your father's request, leaving this up to you..."

I squeezed his hand, encouraging him to keep talking, because I could hear it in the way his words trailed off. There's more he wanted to say. Much more.

"I've been thinking about this a while, and I'm not sure if it would even work." His river-blue eyes reached into mine. "But if you wanted, I could offer myself to the Light for you. I could do what Liander wouldn't and take this burden off your shoulders."

My mother's warning crawled across me, but his eyes seemed so genuine, so caring.

"Not at all to say I don't think you can do it," he added. "I know you,

Ryn. You'll rise to anything. But I hate seeing you so crushed, so worried. And I know it was never your dream."

I couldn't find words to answer. I just stared at him until his hand slipped from mine, and he stood. "Just something to ponder."

The rest of that entry is a storm of thoughts—ending with my genuine consideration of it. But the following pages are riddled with fear. More outbursts. Then eventually, I concluded Verik was unfit to bear the title of Illuminarch with how the nethermagic tainted him. Even if he tried to claim it, the Illuminant would never permit it. Besides, how could he? He's not from the lineage.

Still, the sentiment haunts me now. *Why would he even offer?*

I shut the journal, having quite enough of it, and my gaze drifts to my new companion. He shuffles, probably from the careless way I'd slammed my journal, and a minute later he's sitting, scanning the world around him. I'm the last place he looks, and he turns away just as soon as he sees me.

I should say something. Apologize, perhaps, for going cold on him yesterday, but I don't have the energy to attempt a conversation.

We go through our regular motions, taking turns in the river as soon as the light touches it. I go first, returning with fish that I cook while he washes up. We eat, evading looking each other's way like we're afraid we'll die if we make eye contact.

And I might. Because just the sight of him is shoveling layers of guilt over me. For such a brave and clever man, there's something timid in him when it comes to me. Perhaps it's my heritage. Or just his lack of experience with people. Or the wretched way he was raised. Whichever it is, it makes it hard to keep my shoulder turned against him. As if I'm punishing him for speaking the truth I was too afraid to admit to myself.

But to open my mouth would be worse. I know it. I can't trust my tongue when it's throbbing. I'll say something that might just put him off our whole mission.

Would that really be so bad?

I try to trample the thought as we head out again. But it follows me like a shadow, growing longer the more I try to forget it. It's nothing but fear and weakness stretching it, and yet the temptation to respond to it nibbles at my heels. Even if we make it to the Etherium, don't my former fears still stand? The kingdom will despise me. And what makes me believe I'll be able to do all that awaits me? Raising a new order of Luminors? Defeating Solalé? Ridding the world of netherbeasts? And what if, somehow, the witchlord *does* escape in all this?

The whole mission is a waste. We either die in here or we die facing the future.

Maybe we should go back while we still have our lives.

A sudden sound tumbles me out of my thoughts—the same skidding noise I heard yesterday morning. I look around. *How did it get so late already?* The sun is already partially blocked by the east wall, casting a shadow where we stand.

Dangerous, distracting thoughts, I curse.

My bow is already in Ezro's hand, and his sharp gaze is darting from one direction to the next. Our eyes finally meet again, only to silently confirm we both heard the noise. But from *where?* I see nothing in the shadows.

Same as yesterday.

Ezro nocks an arrow and ventures toward the noise. His steps are as silent as his breaths. I follow behind, not wanting to leave myself standing in the open. We double-scan the premises, behind every boulder and shrub. Every tree.

Nothing.

I turn my sights to the cliff side in case whatever it is can climb, but all that mars the layered stone are a few parched bushes that made the mistake of growing on its ledges.

Where is it?

Ezro and I exchange another glance, but right then, I hear it. *Close.* A noise like heavy bags of sand dragging the ground. What prize did the monster find this time? A bear? Another netherbeast? Will it be dragging us next? Or is it large enough to swallow us whole?

But then I realize something odd about the noise. The dragging is the only sound. Where are the footsteps of the beast itself?

Or is that the noise of the beast?

Tell me it isn't a—

Ezro stops abruptly, throwing his arms out to block me. I nearly crash into him before I see what stilled him.

A black pit.

Graces. It is.

I grab his arm, tugging him away. We creep back until our heels are to the river. Light still shines on the other side, and if not for the white water, I'd suggest we try to brave a swim across.

I finally let go of Ezro's arm, hardly noticing I was still clinging to it, and whisper, "It's beneath us."

His eyes light with realization. "Tunnel wyrm."

I nod.

He steadies the bow toward the pit, and we both watch it. Waiting and waiting. At any moment, the serpentine monster will emerge with scales stronger than steel and venom that can paralyze a man in three seconds. All it would take is one stab from its stinger tail and the fight would be over. Our bodies would soon be sliding, alive, through its long throat until we suffocated.

Of all beasts—

I hear the noise again. Quieter. Has it passed us? Or is it simply choosing a surface point we haven't discovered already?

I shift closer to Ezro, hands burning with the ache to hold the bow he now wields. I should have gone to the academy myself—taken the risk of being discovered. Instead, I'm standing here, worthless.

Pathetic.

Yet something about standing in his shadow is more comforting than I want to admit.

We wait until every trace of sunlight has diminished from the ravine, then finally, Ezro lowers his bow.

"Think it moved on," he says.

"In the direction we need to go."

He stares that way, thumb tapping the bow. "Then we should hang back. Give it a chance to get well ahead of us."

My shoulders tense, but I know—once again—he's right.

"Let's at least get away from his burrow," I suggest.

Ezro agrees, turning back the way we came. We walk until satisfied with our distance, then sling our bags to the ground and make camp—not that anyone could rest knowing a tunnel wyrm is about. Even the other netherbeasts are afraid of them.

No wonder we've seen so few.

Ezro prods at the fresh fire to adjust the sticks. The flames excite, tiny embers sparkling in the air. I watch them rise and die. All burned up.

It's getting hard not to wonder if we'll share the same fate.

Ezro pokes at the fire again, then steps back, eyes gleaming. He tosses the stick and looks at me, almost like he's asking for permission to speak.

But when all I offer is a blank stare, he speaks anyway.

"You should use this as your chance to catch up on some sleep." He nods over to my sprawled blanket. "Know you didn't sleep a minute last night."

"There's a wyrm nearby. I doubt I'll have better luck sleeping now," I say.

"And if it comes close, it'll be a dead wyrm." He gives me a half-hearted smirk. "So sleep."

More like you'll be a dead man.

But I pin my lips closed and plop onto my blanket. I force myself to eat a few handfuls of pine nuts and a sprig-full of blackcurrants. My head sinks against my lumpy bag as I lie down and attempt to shut my eyes. But I suddenly feel my pendant hanging on my neck like it weighs a dozen pounds, and even with the wyrm to worry about, all my mind can do is swell with heart-stabbing thoughts. Strangely, the loudest of them being about Ezro; not Verik at all.

Have I ruined whatever it is we have?

But just as the fear is shallowing my breath, something else occurs to me.

I'm free.

I'm free to worry about what Ezro thinks. To feel what it is I want about him. To want something more. Because if this is true about Verik—that he never loved me—then he didn't die for me at all. He died for his own selfish pursuits. My heart never really was his.

It's still mine. Mine to hold and mine to give as if I'd never handed it to anyone else in the first place.

Like the necromancer's roots snapping off me, I feel the release across my body. Air fills my lungs fully for what feels like the first time in months. I smile all the way inside my heart. And even though I still feel it bleeding from the hole Verik pierced into it, I sense that at last my season of healing has come. My spring. And now it all makes sense why I couldn't progress to it before. I was trapped in the wrong winter, grieving the wrong thing. But now that I understand that, I know what I must let go of—what leaves need to fall—to make way for life to return to me again.

24
EZRO

THE WYRM HOLES MARK EVERY THREE MILES ALONG THE RIVER, AND now I'm wondering how long we've been passing them without noticing. Does the wyrm's tunnel follow the river from one end of the canyon to the other? Has it sensed us up here?

I remember the silence in the room when my netherbeast instructor taught about them at the Bronze Guard Academy. Not only are they one of the largest beasts to enter Paran'dan, they're also some of the hardest to kill. The instructor shared the technique with us, but I distinctly remember that involving multiple people. And all I have is *me*.

Still, I kept myself awake replaying the technique a thousand times in my head and picturing the wyrm falling to my feet. Mother used to say if we watch ourselves succeed enough in our imagination, it's like channeling the success in whatever we're doing. It gives us confidence.

I'm not sure I want to find out if there's anything to it.

I dip an ear toward the third hole we find. Inside is utter silence, which hopefully means it's far ahead of us. Either that or it heard me stepping by and is now waiting for me to turn around so it can strike.

But I walk to the riverside without getting eaten, and we continue on our way.

"I can feel autumn in the air," Vaeryn says.

I jolt at the sound of her voice. Nearly two days of silence outside of necessary exchanges, and that's how she starts a conversation with me again? Talking about the weather?

"Takes longer to reach the south than you're used to," I say.

"Does anything wither in the desert during the colder months?"

I fight to keep my face flat. *What does it matter? Are we just going to ignore the way our last proper conversation went and act like strangers exchanging cheap words over a shop counter?*

"Not really," I say, looking around at the familiar sagebrush. "It's more like the cold just stunts everything."

"But nothing sheds its leaves?"

"A few trees, but mostly no. Doesn't get cold enough, I guess."

She fiddles with her braid, taking her time responding. "That's a shame. In Brïsbrook, the shedding of the forest is one of the most important times of the year. My parents would take Liander and I to the woods and have us each pick out a tree when they first turned gold. We'd tell the tree everything we wanted it to let go of for us—whatever pain we'd gathered in that year. Then we'd watch it shed its leaves, symbolizing to us it was okay to let go. Through winter, the tree would remain barren. My father once said it was because it's necessary to grieve what we've let go of before we're ready to start something new. We spent much of winter mourning, but the moment the green sprouts returned to our tree, we knew that meant our hearts were ready to move on."

I stare at her until I nearly trip on an uneven piece of earth. Is there more to why she's telling me this? *She couldn't be suggesting—*

I dip my head to see if that pendant is still on her neck, but sure enough, the chain is there. Then what does she mean? Is this about the kingdom?

"I'd like to do that again," she says. "Perhaps you'd like to come with me? I'd say we both have much we could offer the trees."

Her meaning slices through me like a sword.

Mother. Niah. The life I thought I had.

Yeah, I could shed a forest.

"It's a little late now, isn't it?" I ask. "Aren't they already shedding?"

"They are just beginning, yes. But I suppose you're right. By the time we've reached the Etherium and could use the portals to go to Brïsbrook, the trees would already be bare or close to it."

The disappointment in her tone gets my gears turning. I look around the canyon. Surely, there'll be a gold tree in here somewhere. I know I've seen a couple scattered along the way, but right now, all I see are evergreens. Those aren't any better than the cacti.

"We could make up something else," I say. "Write things down, toss them into a fire."

A solemn smile stretches her face. "But that lacks the season of mourning. It's too immediate."

"Is it really necessary to cry for three months?" I say it like a joke, but the seriousness returns to her face.

"It's the only way." Her fingertips brush the bark of a pine tree. "Perhaps not three whole months, but however long it takes for the pain to be felt fully."

"Sounds awful."

"It is," she says, but she's smiling again. "Until spring comes."

I'm just thinking about asking her what her idea of spring looks like—and if it has anything to do with me—when I hear the whisper of falling dirt behind us. I snatch my bow and whirl back, and my blood drains into my feet.

Looming taller than my head is a limbless white beast with the face of a dragon. It hisses at us, lashing its slit tongue between a battalion of razor-sharp teeth before it lunges for me.

The wyrm.

25
VAERYN

Ezro and I leap in opposite directions, splitting like a shaft from wheat. The serpentine beast collides teeth-first with the dirt between us. Dust puffs from the impact, clouding the beast's crown of long, curving spikes. The wyrm recoils, head held high above us. Its bone-white scales shine in the shadows. It releases a vehement hiss that curls my toes. *Run,* my instincts scream, but the zip of an arrow as it spits from the bow at my left reminds me I need not run.

At least, not far.

The arrow sinks into the wyrm's pallid throat like a thorn, but nothing more. A mere nuisance to a creature of its size.

Ezro launches another arrow, this one aimed at the wyrm's black eyes, but the beast dodges it, and the arrow falls, useless, into the brush. The wyrm slithers further from its hole, body grating the stone-speckled ground. Its head raises nearly to the treetops as it readies its attack.

My gaze shifts to Ezro, the beast's clear and only target, yet he doesn't move. He holds his arrow steady, watching. I want to scream at him to get behind a tree for shelter. But I don't get beyond the draw of a breath before the wyrm strikes. My body stiffens as if turned to stone, only to ease at the realization that Ezro isn't between the wyrm's teeth but has dashed behind the beast.

His arrow flies and penetrates the soft skin behind the wyrm's jaw. Fury loudens the wyrm's hiss as it snaps its attention toward him. *Now*, Ezro runs. The wyrm slithers after him, its full form quickly unearthing from the hole. I trail well behind as the wyrm weaves through the trees like thread carried behind a needle. Through fleeting glimpses, I catch Ezro tucking his bow away, exchanging it for his quarterstaff, which he assembles with a sharp twist.

What in the lands does he think he's going to do with that against this beast?

Again, my mouth opens to insert myself, and is promptly stunned to silence when he swirls around to face the wyrm. He's met by a mouth of snapping teeth that he narrowly dodges before he might have lost a leg. The metal staff hammers against the beast's mouth—provoking it into another strike. This, Ezro catches with the end of his staff held against the roof of the wyrm's mouth. Saliva drips from the pointed ends of the wyrm's teeth like dripping icicles. The wyrm's weight bears down, pushing Ezro back and back, until finally, it retracts. For a split second, its dark eyes turn to me, as if to weigh my threat before it determines me worthless. It snaps after Ezro again.

Their fight turns into a swift sequence of strikes and dodges, hits and hisses. Then suddenly, Ezro wedges his staff into the wyrm's mouth, holding it wide. The wyrm writhes back, whipping its head from side to side in a vain attempt to toss the staff. Ezro grabs his bow and lines it with an arrow. He watches the wild motions of the beast and releases his arrow with blood-chilling precision. The arrow sails into the wyrm's mouth, planting into the back of its throat. Ezro grabs another, repeating the process as many times as it takes before the hits render lethal. The wyrm hisses one last time and flumps to the ground.

Heart throbbing, I face Ezro to see the corners of his lips crawling to a smile. His wide eyes bat as he stares at his fallen enemy. I scan over him for damage, finding he sustained only a couple of nicks from branches he must have brushed against in his flight. *Incredible.*

"You're sure you don't have experience fighting monsters?" I ask to draw his attention to me. Something unwanted flutters in my stomach when his smile spreads even more.

"I do now," he says.

I pin my lips flat, not wanting to feed into his confidence too much.

He pries the staff from the beast's mouth and holds it out. Slimy wyrm spit slides down the shaft and globs to the ground. He glances about like he's looking for something to wipe it on besides himself, but just as his eyes set on the river, the wyrm twitches. I squeak a warning as the wyrm's stinger tail loops toward him and strikes him in the side.

His eyes bulge, the color draining from his face. His enemy drops. Stinging him, its final act.

Ezro tilts.

I bolt after him, but I'm not quick enough to catch him before he slams to the ground. I gape at the hole in the side of his leather armor where the stinger penetrated. Blood and venom froth from it, souring my stomach at the sight. I reach for my bag, hoping I have something left to help him, but as I unbuckle the strap, a low groan turns my eyes toward the trees.

Then I hear a rustle in the opposite direction.

Netherbeasts. Graces, the battle must have lured them.

My heart leaps into my throat. The venom shouldn't kill him. *Shouldn't.* But the other beasts would be happy to while he's unconscious.

Shaking, I frantically search my surroundings for a place to hide us. The sun is still on the other side of the river, but how would I get him across?

Another rumble clenches my teeth. *Where—?*

Wait.

I spin toward the hole the wyrm emerged from. Nothing else would dare go in there. *I hope.*

I rise, swiftly gathering and disassembling Ezro's slimy staff before shoving each end into his backpack. Loaded with both our bags, I wipe my hands dry against my cloak and roll Ezro onto his back. His body plops as if dead, but his wheezy breaths assure me otherwise. I grab his wrists and heave, dragging him across the bumpy ground as the beastly noises rumble closer.

Sweat beads on my neck from the stress and effort. My eyes never stop checking my sides. Utterly defenseless. That's what we are. Unless Raphós, by some unlikely miracle, decided to come to our aid. But he seems to have long forgotten me. It's been weeks since he's appeared to my rescue.

A rustle of leaves turns my head toward a trembling bush. I go still, watching. Waiting. Nothing comes of it. I pull Ezro's limp body on.

How long will he be like this? Will the tunnels really stay safe?
What if there's another wyrm down there?

Every question raises my pulse. How did I ever think I could do this alone before?

Finally, I approach the tunnel entrance. I check behind me again. Nothing seems to be watching from what I can see. I tug Ezro across the final stretch, cringing at the multitude of rocks scraping against him, then let his hands down so I can scope the inside first.

I retrieve my lantern and ease inside, spine leaned back to fight the steep slope as I walk down. Several paces into the dirt encasing, I feel the ground leveling out until I can stand completely upright.

I nod to myself, assured this is the safest place we can go. Though dark, no other creatures would brave the passages of these territorial beasts.

Not until they discover it dead.

"*If* they do," I whisper to myself, wishing Ezro had been awake to say it to me.

I hurry back up the slant, nerves already jittering at the matter of seconds it's been since he was in my sight. My mind plays horrible visions of me surfacing to find him already torn apart or in the clutches of another beast I'd be helpless against, but when I peek my head out, he's lying where I left him.

I sigh and muster my strength to yank him into shelter. Two good tugs and the slope sends him sliding to the bottom. I wince again. *I hope he's as unconscious as he looks.*

I drag him deeper in until the glow of my lantern no longer touches the exit. Then I lay him down with his backpack propped beneath his head. I dig through my bag with tingling hands until I find my medicine pack. I drop to my knees, hurriedly unstrapping his breastplate and rolling his shirt away from the effervescent wound. From what little I know of treating it, a heap of broadleaf balm pressed into the lesion and good stitching should handle the puncture and begin neutralizing the venom.

I feel through my supplies until my fingers land on a cool metal tin. With a quick twist of the cap, the potent, almost peppery scent floods the tight enclosure.

"I don't suppose you can hear me," I say. "But if somehow you can, I'm terribly sorry for this."

I sink my fingers into the salve.

26

VAERYN

A GROAN SHAKES THE CREEPING SLUMBER OFF ME, AND I TWIST, HAIR falling loose from my disheveled braid. Across from me, Ezro lies, staring at the dirt ceiling with a crease in his brow. His hand lifts, then plops to the ground, and he groans again.

I lean off the wall where I'd propped myself and bring the lantern closer to him. The light reveals deep purple rings around his eyes, and I can't help but frown. He looks worse than the last time I checked on him; except for the fact that he's awake now, boggling at me like he's never seen me before.

I kneel at his side, trying to smile despite the anxiety shortening my breath. "Are you sore?" I ask.

He doesn't even blink.

"Ezro?" I ask louder. "Are you sore?"

Another long pause unfolds before he croaks, "Vaeryn?"

"Who else would be here with you?"

A lazy smile crawls onto his face, tearing fresh the split in his lip from his fall. But his gaze drifts back to the ceiling. "Where's the sky?"

"Behind all this dirt," I say, settling on the ground with my legs bent to my side. "We're inside the wyrm's tunnel. The one that stung you. Do you remember?"

His long, befuddled look suggests not.

"It attacked us, and you shot it down with your arrows. It fell as though dead but found some remnant of energy to get revenge. It stung you, right there, in your side." I point, but the ceiling entrances his eyes. "It died right after, but other netherbeasts were around, so I dragged you in here where we should be safe."

He tries to lift his hand again and, this time, it makes it into his tousled hair. He rustles it around, only making it messier than it was before.

"Do you want to try sitting up?" I ask.

His gaze shifts back to me, and another empty stare overtakes him for several moments before he remembers to respond. "Yeah."

He reaches for me and I grab his hand, but my gentle tug does nothing to sit him up. I grab his forearm with my other hand and hoist him upright—only for him to tilt sideways. A soft yelp escapes my lips as I reach after him, catching him just below the shoulders. I steady him, uncertain if I can trust him not to topple again if I let go, but now stuck with him gaping at me from an arm's length away.

My throat goes dry. Even sickly looking, those warm eyes still stir a flutter inside my chest. Especially as he gives me another wide, if delirious, smile.

I clear my throat after an extensive moment of not knowing what to do. "I suppose we are even now. You tended to me in my weakness that day in the heat..." I look behind him. "Perhaps we should get you closer to the wall. Let that hold you up."

I stand and awkwardly maneuver myself behind him so I can hook my hands beneath his arms and pull him a few inches further. I sidestep and lean him against the dirt wall. Once he seems stable—physically, at least—I return to my place on the opposite wall and sit.

"You glow in here," he says, his tone higher and lazier than I've ever heard it. The way he sways worries me that he'll tip over again at any moment. "Like looking at the moon."

I glance at my pale arms and ivory braid, then back to his much warmer features. His irises seem to gather all the light from the lantern's glow, shining themselves in the same gold as the flame.

"And you're the sun." The thought escapes my lips unwittingly, and regret pinches my stomach. I offer him a friendly smile, hoping to cover it as a polite return of compliment and nothing more.

"I'd rather look at the moon."

My nails tap against my knee. "Well, there wouldn't be much of a moon to look at if the sun wasn't there."

A soft chuckle shirks his shoulders and fades. For a moment, a deeper silence than I've ever known oppresses my ears. But then his voice scatters it again. "I'm not going anywhere," he says. "Not until I see you on that throne."

"And then?"

"You tell me, Illuminarch."

Heat blooms across my face. What did I ever do to deserve such loyalty?

He waits for my answer with a growing exhaustion that makes me doubt he'll even remember this conversation in a few hours. And that doubt makes me foolish enough to try my honest answer.

"You stay."

His head inclines to the side.

"In my life."

The usual tension eases back onto his face, but he remains quiet. I catch myself fidgeting with the tie on my blouse.

"I want you to be one of my Luminors," I say, hoping to answer the question he's not asking.

His eyelids bat, a faraway look making me uncertain if he'd heard my answer at all or if it threw him into another form of shock. But then he pitches to the side, and before I can reach him, he hits the ground again.

I wake from a brief nap a few hours later and find Ezro awake again. Awake and shaking. Panic wipes away my grogginess, and I lurch to his side. His shrunken pupils stay affixed ahead of him, barely aware of my presence. I press the back of my hand against his forehead and cheek, and his skin blazes against my own. My hand retracts, and another surge of terror freezes me in place.

I thought Father said wyrm venom only stunned its victims? Why is he burning with a fever? How long has he been like this?

I rush for my supplies and quickly dampen a cloth. I lay it across his forehead, then check the puncture in his side for infection. The stitched wound shows no sign of it, just a hint of crusted blood.

"Ezro?"

Several moments later, he looks at me as his only answer.

"You need to sip some water. I need to sit you back up," I say.

He responds with a low, one-measure hum. I take it for compliance and wrestle him upright, hoping he can manage to sit against the wall long enough to hydrate. He holds steady, clutching his arms as he shivers.

The paralysis is wearing off, at least.

I retrieve his canteen, unscrew the cap, and hand it to him. He manages to drink it alone—praise the Illuminant—and sits, holding it in his lap with his head hung and eyes glazed over. But he continues to sip at the water for a while, and slowly, attentiveness returns to his face. He looks at me, and I realize I'm staring at him like he's sitting in his grave.

"This is good," he says, voice ragged.

"What is?"

"The fever."

I wait through another sip for him to explain.

"Means my body's fighting it off. Be better soon."

The anxiety melts from my face, but not my heart. At least *some-*

one knows something about the way this venom works.

"Do you think you could eat?"

His thumb rubs the rim of his canteen. "Probably not."

I almost offer to make tea, but then remember where we are and where I'd have to go to prepare it. I sigh, weary to my bones with feeling helpless. "Is there anything I can do?"

He sits with my question for a long while, body quivering. The sight twists my stomach with worry, despite his assurance that he'll recover soon. What if he doesn't? What if he dies right here in these tunnels? What if I'm left here alone in the middle of the canyon?

What would that matter? I'd die of guilt before the netherbeasts ever discovered me.

"Just stay close," he says, shifting to lie down again. "That way, I know you're safe."

I swallow, wishing I possessed the nerve to ask why he cares. Is it only because of the blood in my veins, or is there something more to his concern?

The chiseled shadows across his face rearrange as he smiles at me one last time and turns onto his back. His eyes close and he goes still besides the occasional shudder. I watch for a while, strangled with the lonely thought of sitting here in this deafening silence again. Eventually, I recall that I still have one last page left in my journal. I adjust the light and settle in to fill every line.

27

EZRO

I THOUGHT YOU'D BE THE SON MY FATHER ALWAYS WANTED.

Father's words find me in my sleep. They echo until they weave into a memory where I'm hammering a blunt blade in Grandfather's smithy. Grandfather watches me, close. His presence is as hot and dangerous as the forge itself. And I'm small; head reaching barely to his shoulders.

"Your father told me you were strong," Grandfather says, then he snorts and snatches the hammer from my hand. He pounds the steel blade, every hit like a crack of thunder. I watch the blade straightening, thinning, wondering how he expects me to do that when his biceps are as wide as my head.

He shoves the hammer against my chest, hard enough to stagger the breath in my lungs. I grip the hammer and try again, hitting the blade with all my might. The impact rings as loud as his, and I'm just thinking to smile when I notice a crack snaking down the metal like a bolt of lightning.

"*Boy!*" Grandfather yells, pushing me in the shoulder. I stumble sideways, the hammer fumbling from my grip. It thuds to the floor, and I fight the urge to flee to the far side of the shop, to run out the door, to get somewhere high. But then I'll hear it again: *Act like that and I'm sending you back to your father.*

But that would mean I failed Niah. She'd be stuck in Jarden, vulnerable to the netherbeasts, and I'd be to blame for it. So, I plant my feet as his heavy steps pound toward me, shutting my eyes at the raise of his hand. I picture Niah to hide from what happens next, and her laughing in a field of late spring flowers shelters me like armor.

But when I reopen my eyes, it's not Grandfather I see. It's a different version of Niah. The version of her standing in our dim hallway with beads of water dripping off her limp hair.

"I'm sorry," I say, but resentment still burns me from her gaze.

I repeat it again. And again. Each time growing more desperate, more pathetic until suddenly a different voice answers—a gentle *shush.*

My brows cave, and I turn, expecting to see my mother standing behind me.

But instead of her dark waves, I see strands of white. White as pure as moonlight.

"It's okay."

I jolt awake, finding the same white hair pouring over Vaeryn's shoulders. Unbraided, for the first time that I've seen it. Then I register her backhand pressed to my forehead, but only for a second before she recoils a whole leap away.

"It is a wonder you're even alive for how poorly you always sleep," she says. "But it seems your fever has passed."

I push myself upright, feeling the weakness in my joints and a sharp sting in my left side. Serves me right for being proud of defeating that wyrm.

Vaeryn hands me my canteen. "How do you feel?"

I gulp what little remains of my water. "Like I'm tired of lying around."

"Why does that answer incline me to tell you to go back to sleep?"

I smile and use the wall to support myself as I stand. Instantly, I feel the tremble in my knees, but I force myself straight. I'd rather fumble through these tunnels than go back to my nightmares. Doesn't matter how sick I am.

"Think these tunnels run all the way through the canyon?" I ask, slinging my bag over my shoulder.

Vaeryn grimaces but follows my lead despite herself. "No telling. But wouldn't that be a stroke of good luck?"

"Only way to find out is to follow it, right?"

I look each way, wondering which leads forward since all I see in either direction is perpetual darkness. Vaeryn swoops up the lamp and starts walking. I fall into step at her side, feeling every stride like I'm wading through high water. We'd better hope nothing else comes down here, because right now, I'm not sure if I could even draw the string of my bow.

We walk at least thirty minutes before a halo of light emerges ahead. Vaeryn rushes down the off-shoot and peers outside, then comes half-skidding down the steep slope to the exit.

"We're right by the river. There's plenty of sun," she says. "Let's go up for air."

I stare into the dark passage, impatient to see if my battle with the wyrm earned us a shortcut to the Etherium, but the empty canteen hanging at my waist reminds me I don't have much choice.

I follow her up the slant, irritated at how exhausted I feel by the time I'm surfacing in the ravine. The sunlight stings my eyes, but the fresh breeze in my hair makes me forget about the tunnels almost instantly.

I fill my canteen in the river and splash the cool water into my face. It sends a chill over me—like a threat of the fever's return—and I scowl, casting every insult I can think of in the direction of that giant, dead wyrm. I can't be weak. Not here in this canyon. Not with the Illuminarch counting on me to keep her alive.

I turn to check for her and find her staring at the pine trees like they're talking to her. I always heard people from the north had a thing about trees, but I'm only just catching on to why.

I never answered her about her miserable autumn ritual.

But now that I'm thinking of it again, I can't help but wonder if it would help *me*. Even if all it did was stop the nightmares, that would be something.

"What are they saying?" I ask.

Vaeryn turns toward me, and the breeze flutters her loose hair from her face. It resettles against her ever-flushed cheeks, framing her elegant features.

"What do you mean?" she asks.

My mind goes blank staring at her beauty. *What were we talking about?*

"The trees," I say when it hits me. I close the distance between us, joining her in between a near perfect circuit of evergreens. "You looked pretty intent on them. Like you were listening to them talk. You northerners and your trees."

"You mean the cacti don't tell you their memories?" she asks.

My forehead crinkles before I realize it was a joke.

She chuckles, tilting her head up again. "I'm just soaking in the sight of them after a full day in the dirt and darkness; it's an even more lovely sight than I remembered. I suggest you appreciate them too, while you have the chance. We could be in those tunnels for a long while. Who knows how frequent the exits will be?"

I follow her gaze but find the prickly branches far less fascinating than the sight of her admiring them. But the longer I indulge, the deeper anxiety nestles into my being. Even if the tunnels get us to the portal, I'd never expect to walk straight to it. No. Netherbeasts will swarm it. Ones like the wyrm, larger than houses. And every last one of them will want us dead. Especially her.

Vaeryn is like a precious flame I'm taking straight into a windstorm, doing all I can to keep the gusts from putting her out. But how could I ever be enough?

My stomach burns. A thought I'd somehow never considered crossing my mind. *What if I survive, and she doesn't?*

I turn my back, alarmed at how quickly the thought makes my

eyes sting. I blink myself back to normal and blame it on the venom still compromising me. But deep down, I know it has nothing to do with the venom. It has to do with her voice being the one that breaks through my nightmares and sends me into peaceful sleep. With her eyes feeling like the only safe place left in this entire world. With her trust instilling in me the first taste of real confidence and worth I've had since Mother was alive.

Illuminant, help me keep her alive, I pray, and though I've prayed it a thousand times, I feel it like a knife through my chest. A knife that will dig deeper every single day we spend together.

A sprinkle of yellow through all the green catches my eyes. I squint, realizing there's a yellowing tree near the river. The sight reminds me once again of what I was trying to bring up.

"Do we have to watch the leaves fall off for it to work?" I ask.

She gives me a puzzled look, and I nod her toward the tree.

Her brows lift with her smile. "An oak?"

I snort a laugh. *Of course she'd know what it is, even from this far away.*

"The point is to watch it shed, yes." She starts toward it. "But perhaps just knowing it will happen will be enough. Besides, you should see it up close."

I follow behind her enlivened steps, an odd nervousness sneaking up my spine. All I have to do is tell the tree everything I want to let go of.

But has anyone ever named their entire life before?

The oak tree's trunk is thicker than any I've ever seen. Its branches loom high above my head in some places, but others dip low enough to make me duck. Most of the wide leaves are still green with yellow tips as if someone dipped them in paint, but a few leaves are already withered on the ground. I crunch one beneath my boot, smiling at the satisfying sound. When I move my foot, all that remains is the leaf's skeleton. The rest is crumbled in the dirt. I try to picture that it's one of the things I'm letting go of—Father's words that replayed in my head all through my sleep.

If only their effects could crumble as easily as this leaf.

This is pointless.

I should have let us return to the tunnels without saying a word about this stupid tree, but Vaeryn is too resolved for me to back out now.

"You go first," I say.

Vaeryn's expression turns somber, but she nods and steps to the base of the tree. Her fingertips run along the dense bark, and I hear the faintest whisper. I try not to listen, but I can't help it. She didn't say I *couldn't*, and I want to know if she's decided to let Verik go, or if she plans on harboring guilt over his death forever.

I incline my ear toward her, throwing my gaze to the pointed pine tops. I catch his name but can't hear much else besides a mention of her brother, Liander, and their mother.

"Okay." Her voice is suddenly much louder. "Now you tell it what you need, then we'll finish it together."

I frown, but at this point, anything is worth trying. And if I don't do it, I sense Vaeryn will judge me for the rest of my life—however short it may be.

I approach the tree but stand a full step further away than she had. "Do I have to touch it?"

She chuckles. "Only if you want."

I leave my hands at my sides. My lungs feel like pockets full of stones. I search for the right place to begin, but even when I find it, I'm not sure how to say it. "How much am I supposed to tell it?"

"As much or as little as you want. There are no rules, really."

I consider it awhile, then decide to simply list it off. "Mother's death. Father sending me to Fenfyre, knowing how Grandfather would treat me. Having this mark forced on me. Everything Grandfather did. All the people I wanted to know but wasn't allowed to. Learning it was Niah who turned Mother in and—" My voice breaks, and I unwittingly find my hand on the tree, supporting me. There's so much more to say, and yet, I can feel it—the brewing tears, lump in my throat. If I speak them, I'll be crying right here at this tree with

Vaeryn here to watch it.

Your Father told me you were strong. Grandfather's voice sneaks into my head again, but now, his context feels different. He's not judging my arms, but my heart. *Weak.* That's how I look now. Having to hold myself up by this tree. Too pathetic to speak the words to hand over to it. Not to mention the venom still sapping my energy, which should have never happened. Why didn't I see the stinger coming? Didn't I learn about that at the academy?

"Training with Bronze Guards, with my enemies," I add to the list. "And serving them in the smithy."

My thoughts return to Niah, a surge of emotion rising in my chest. But what more do I say about her? What do I let go of? Who I thought she was? The care I thought she had for me? What she said?

It feels so raw thinking on it again, as though I've avoided the wound all this time, and it's still bleeding under the surface.

"Niah," I finally decide to say, figuring her name will cover it all. "And Father threatening to turn me in as if my death was better than him having to see me again."

I look to Vaeryn, expecting to see judgment in her eyes, but if anything, she looks sadder than I've ever seen her.

"Now what?" I ask.

She steps beside me and lays one hand on the bark and the other rests against my nearly healed shoulder. Her eyes shine as she looks up the tall trunk into the sturdy branches.

"To my family, this isn't just a tree," she says. "It represents the Illuminant. This practice was started by the Faithful many years ago, but over time, his name was left out." Her gaze meets mine again, sunlight from between the branches splotching her face in light and shadow. "We have just surrendered it all into his hands. He will now bear with us the suffering, the shedding, and then he will bring the healing."

She smiles, whispering a quiet thanks to the Illuminant before meeting my gaze again. "I'm proud of you," she says, then her hand slips off my shoulder, and she turns back for the tunnels.

28

EZRO

"Have you decided yet if you'd like to be a Luminor?" Vaeryn asks me the next day as we're traveling through the endless darkness.

"I didn't realize that was an option," I say, holding up the makeshift torch we've exchanged for our dried-out lanterns.

"I mentioned it while you were recovering."

I shake my head. "I don't remember it. Hardly remember anything that happened."

Several paces separate my response from hers. "Well, I thought since you are doing all this for me, it seems fair to offer you a place as one of my Luminors."

I stare down the throat of the tunnel, wondering what she hopes I'll say. Does she *want* me to be one, or is she only offering because it's the right thing to do?

"Would the Illuminant even allow it?" I ask.

"Why wouldn't he?"

I twist my bronze crescent into her view. "I'm marked with nethermagic. Why would he let a Bronze Guard become a Luminor? I'd be surprised if—"

Suddenly, my entire body freezes over, stopping me in my tracks.

Vaeryn faces me, an expectant, nervous squint in her eye.

"—if I can even go through the portal," I finish, and what I intended as an exaggeration suddenly feels like a realization.

"What?"

I delay my answer until I can muster the strength to swim myself from the tidal wave of terror that's just crashed over me. "You said nothing of the netherworld can go through the portal."

"You're not a netherbeast—"

"But there is nethermagic inside me," I say, holding the mark up again.

"A drop of it."

"What's the difference?" I ask. "The Etherium is a sacred place. Why should I expect to enter it with this? I'll probably be incinerated if I even try."

Vaeryn's hand presses to her forehead and she turns away. "*Graces…* You don't really think…"

"If that doesn't do it, I'm sure you anointing me will. So maybe we shouldn't try."

"But it's not your fault that you have that mark." Her gaze returns to me again. "You didn't choose that. They forced you to receive it as a child. The Illuminant should cleanse you of it for stepping through the portal, not *incinerate* you. Ezro, you can't—"

"But it's not just that," I cut in, panic swelling my chest. "It's worse."

"What do you mean?"

The torch's flickering flames reflect in her eyes, and I wish they could burn my entire history away. The tree's done nothing. Absolutely nothing for how I feel.

"I've got bad blood," I say.

She steps nearer, the opposite of what I expect her to do, and narrows her eyes at me. "What makes you say that?"

"My family has served Solalé since her reign, helping her and her

Bronze Guards. The same people who murder the Faithful. Vaeryn, even if I never got this mark, it's in my blood. I'm one of them—"

"Ezro." She leaves my name hanging too long. "Whatever bad blood runs in your family's veins; it isn't in you."

"That day with the necromancer's staff. I almost gave in, Vaeryn." I twist away from her. "I was so close. I wanted the power, the attention. It took everything in me not to cave. And that day when my grandfather fired me, I wanted to shoot him. Hurt him. Make him pay for everything—that's the type of person I really am."

For the longest time, the torch's soft chortle is the only sound, then Vaeryn takes another step toward me. "Those scars on you—I've seen them. Your grandfather did that, all of it, didn't he?"

My grip constricts around the torch, knocking ashes to my feet. We need to go back up soon, or we'll be swallowed in darkness. But maybe that would be better. Then she couldn't see my pulsing temple or read the secrets in my eyes.

She speaks again without my answer. "You are not a bad person because you wished justice upon the wicked. One might call you merciful for reserving it. And just because you were tempted to do evil, doesn't mean you *are* evil. You overcame it—*that's* who you are." She smiles, as tenderly as my mother used to. "I am proud to bring you with me to the Etherium and would be honored to have you as one of my Luminors. I don't care whose family you're from. If anything, it takes more strength for a tree to rise from the harshness of a desert than the abundance of the woods."

Another clump of ash falls to the floor, but my eyes don't turn away for as long as Vaeryn will hold my gaze. If not for that pendant still dangling on her neck, I'd wonder what infatuation caused her to pass over everything I just said like a stone skipping over water. But no. She's still wearing it, which means she didn't let Verik go at the tree. Her heart is still his. It may always be.

So where is this coming from?

She couldn't really mean it, could she?

"Thank you. Really. But let's just take this one step at a time. Ask me again if I make it through the portal." I glance at the fading torch. "Better get back up there. Torch is dying."

29
EZRO

Another week in the safety of the tunnels passes before we reach the center of the canyon. But instead of the sunlight I expected to lead us through our final stretch, there is lightning. Dark clouds. Wind that sweeps between the ravine and quakes every branch and blade of grass. It hits my face like a realization. An awakening. And I feel alive in a way I never have.

Like this is the last day I'll ever live.

"Let's get this done," I say to Vaeryn, taking the first step toward the eastern cavity where the portal supposedly awaits.

Vaeryn's feet stay planted by the river, the gusts sparkling a mist around her. The wind has already pulled strands from her tightly woven braid. They sway over her eyes, untouched, as she stares at me.

"If the passage rejects you, what will you do?" she asks.

"Take the tunnels back out, I guess," I say. *Provided its rejection is more like a locked door than a blazing fire.*

"And then?"

"I don't know," I say, motioning her to follow me. "That's the last thing you need to be worried about. You're about to go accept the responsibility of saving the entire kingdom."

She steps nearer, lightning flashing at her back. "I'll need to know where to find you so I can find some other way to repay you."

"Just get rid of the beasts and Solalé," I say.

"But where will you go?"

I avert my gaze. "I have no idea."

She leaves a long pause. "Well, let's just hope it doesn't come to that."

Don't worry—I'll be dead.

I don't know what makes me so certain of it. Maybe it's the storm. I was born during one of the worst storms Jarden had ever seen. Makes sense that I would die in one. But somehow I feel peace about it. If I die getting Vaeryn to the Etherium, at least it counted for something.

"Come on," I say. "Looks like it's just a mile or two. We might make it before the rain if we hurry."

I start walking again, only for her to grip my arm. I turn. Her hand stays where it is, her face near enough for me to see my own reflection in her irises.

"Please, wait," she says, her hand slipping away. "I'm not ready."

I search her face, trying to discern why after all this way. "What's wrong?"

Her eyes redden the longer she looks at me, a sheen filling them that she swiftly tries to hide by turning her head. I act like I don't notice for the sake of her pride and wait for the woman who shoved her boot to my throat to resurface. The woman who lasted five months alone traveling across the kingdom. Who pulled me from the river when a dozen wraiths were trying to drown me and dragged my paralyzed body into the depths of the world to keep me safe.

And slowly, she comes back. Chin held with rightful royal dignity. Eyes sharp as her mouth. Armored shoulders squared to face whatever threats might await us.

"Pray with me," she says, raising her hands for me to take.

I lay mine in hers, her warm skin tingling my palms. The feeling hurtles me back to my childhood, holding my mother's hands each night before bed as she whispered a prayer over me. And in the pause before Vaeryn speaks, I can almost hear Mother's voice.

Illuminant, be with my son. Guard his heart and mind against all lies. Lead him to the Light. Use him. Please, use him.

"For what?" I'd once asked.

She'd squeezed my hands tighter, a warmth in her smile. "That's for him to decide."

But when Vaeryn speaks, her voice is not a soft whisper like my mother's. It rings clear above the whooshing wind and dances over the thunder.

"Illuminant, you are with us. Your Light is in my blood, and where the Light goes, the darkness cannot follow. May the Light within me protect us both. May it be as though the Light flowed in Ezro's veins just as much as mine. This I ask and by faith receive. You have brought us here and you will see us through to the end."

Her palms slide from mine, and she smiles at me, transformed entirely back to the woman I first met.

"Now then," she says. "To the Etherium."

30

EZRO

Raindrops splatter against the map as Vaeryn holds it between us. Everything looks correct around us. The formation of the walls in the cavity. The distance from the river. The size of the ravine. Everything—except that Vaeryn's map doesn't show a lake, and yet one sprawls before us, directly where our portal is supposed to be.

"It *is* old," Vaeryn says, rolling the map. "I suppose it's not impossible that a lake could have formed here since Father drew this. We should have a look around. Perhaps he means this general area and not…exactly there."

My gaze lingers on the water. Dozens of little wavelets appear and vanish as the clouds begin making their deposit. "I bet the portal is inside it."

"The lake?"

"At the bottom."

She frowns, looking through the trees that hem the lake. "Well, it wouldn't hurt to look on land first before diving in there."

"We're gonna get wet anyway," I say.

"There could be wraiths."

That shuts me up after my last experience with them. I follow her lead around the lake's perimeter, scanning the surroundings for anything that seems unusual. But the only thing that doesn't look right to me is the absence of netherbeasts. The whole way here, Vaeryn's warned me that the portal would be guarded, and yet the only thing assailing us is the steadily increasing rain.

"Maybe we *are* in the wrong place," I say after we've walked halfway around the lake. "Things should be attacking us, shouldn't they?"

She sweeps her gaze in all directions. "So I thought."

We continue around the lake until we're back where we started. Mud already cakes my boots and rain drips from my hood, but still, we've found nothing that seems like a portal to another realm. How could it be so discreet?

"Would be nice if we knew what we were looking for," I mumble.

"Let's try along the canyon wall. If it's not there, then the lake may well be where it is."

Thunder booms overhead as we walk, the walls amplifying it to a near-deafening volume. Lightning webs through the sky in vehement bolts that make me grateful we're not up on the ridges. But the heavy rainfall is pooling at our feet. The whole ground will be the lake before too long.

We rush to the walls and inspect their streaming surface. I pick at cracks and shove anything that faintly resembles a door, but another thirty minutes of downpour later, we've still found nothing. I sigh, accepting my fate for what it is.

I'm jumping into that lake, and now it's even deeper than it was when we got here.

We trudge to it like defeated soldiers, both stopping at the edge. The rain splatter sounds like applause against its greenish surface, like what comes next is pure entertainment to nature. I can't help but scowl at it. I reach for my quiver to unbuckle it, but the plunk of

Vaeryn's bag hitting the ground stills my fingers.

"What do you think *you're* doing?" I ask.

She tackles her cloak next, letting it fall into the mud. "If there are wraiths, then you'd better be on land with your bow."

"*If there are wraiths*, then better me get dragged down than you."

She props her boot against a stone and unravels the knot in a single pull. "I will know the portal when I find it. I believe that. You, I'm not so sure."

"What's that supposed to mean?"

"Just that my ancestors knew it and their blood is in my veins." Her boot plunks beside her cloak and bag.

I toss my backpack down. "Exactly. You're the next Illuminarch, so you need to stay alive."

"Then shoot fast if I'm attacked."

"Can't shoot an arrow to the bottom of the lake." I stamp my boot against a tree to untie it, but she's already removed her second boot and is tossing her blades. Her head snaps in my direction when my laces flap loose, a grimace that could scare my grandfather twisted on her lips.

"Listen to me, Ezro Valorian. If *you* go in this lake to die, then *I* will be left out here in the canyon to the same fate. If *I* die in the lake, at least you still can fight your way back home. One of us must test these waters, and it will not be you, lest I have to bind you to a tree."

"That would make it much harder to save you."

"Then cooperate."

I breathe in rain and dread, then tie up my boot. "Fine."

"Very well."

She faces the lake, rainwater already soaking her clothes. I detach the quiver from my backpack, strap it over me, and ready my bow. My breaths shake, and I realize I'm unprepared for this. To watch her disappear into the water and maybe not come back. Our Illuminarch. My friend.

How did I let her talk me into standing by?

Pauldrons and arm guards splash to the flooded ground as she begins removing her armor. I turn, leaving her to do the rest without my watching. I hear the splat from what must be her leather cuirass, but just as her belt buckle jangles, there is a loud slosh from the lake.

I whirl around just fast enough to see a massive claw as it clamps over her body and yanks her in.

31
EZRO

Thunder smothers my scream as I run to the edge of the lake. I hold an arrow, scanning the sloshing water for the beast. The lake settles, like a rippling pane of glass reflecting the flashing sky. My head throbs. *This can't happen. This can't.*

I lower my arrow and release another worthless scream into the storm. The world teeters.

Again. It's happening *again.* I'm losing someone else. Someone I swore to protect.

I sink the arrow back into its quiver. *No, I'm not. I'm getting her back. I'm going in.*

I reach to untie my boots, but I don't touch them before the water starts churning. I stagger backward, snatching another arrow. I line it on my bow, igniting it with power just as a monstrous beast bursts from the center of the lake. Water rushes through the jagged shells that compose his arthropodan armor, the liquid taking a man-like shape beneath it. A golem of some kind, I guess, but not one I've ever seen in the textbooks.

The lake level lowers as the golem absorbs the water, growing larger by the second. He grows until half the lake is held in his form. The rest is still too deep for me to wade through.

I squint at his long, crustacean fingers, expecting to see Vaeryn trapped inside them. But his hands are empty.

The rain suddenly feels like sleet. *Where is she?*

Her name flies from my lips again, and the aquatic monster hones in on me. I draw my bow, searching for a target. But where? What good will my arrow do to water? And what could penetrate his armor?

I send the arrow into his liquid throat, just to test it. The arrow passes through, doing no more than provoking a spine-straightening roar. My heels dig down, my hand fumbling for another futile arrow. I launch it toward an eye, only for a wave to hurtle from the lake and slap my arrow into its depths.

My fingers go numb. How am I supposed to kill something I can't hurt?

I suddenly have a new appreciation for Vaeryn's tenacity over the last five months.

But *where* is she?

The sound of rushing water rattles the atmosphere. All around the monster, vortices rise from the lake. The liquid twisters consume the rest of the water, leaving nothing but silt and massive bones on the bed. *So* that's *where the rest of the netherbeasts went.*

As my gaze scours between the wobbling liquid pillars for Vaeryn, I see a faint glow, like a window beneath an arch of stone.

The portal.

Everything snaps together in my mind in a single blink. The map didn't show the lake because it *isn't* one. It's a netherbeast.

A cough jerks my attention to the left, but I barely have time to spot Vaeryn's slumped figure in the lakebed before a whirlpool sweeps toward me and smashes into my side. My shoulder crashes into the mud, grip nearly breaking from my bow. I fasten my hold, scrambling up as fast as I'm able.

"Vaeryn! The portal! Go!"

My words hardly escape my lips before I'm knocked over by another vortex. I catch myself, gashing my palm on a rock. The sharp sting is nothing compared to the pain coming if I don't get out of here.

Where is Raphós?

I glance back to Vaeryn, hoping to see her racing for the portal, but she still hasn't moved.

"Go!" I yell at her again and sprint for the trees.

Pillars of water lash at me like whips from each side, but the steady tree trunks break their momentum. The monster's virulent snarl chases behind me, soon followed by the loud snaps of breaking trees. I peer back. His watery, tentacle legs dwindle the space between us at a vicious speed. I hasten my strides, the slippery ground threatening my every step.

But Vaeryn is safe. He's following *me*.

She's going to make it.

And I was right. I was born in a storm. Now I'll die in one.

It almost seems foolish to keep running. Every time I glance back, he's grown from absorbing the rain. Now, he's as tall as the evergreens. I'll never outrun him. I'm just delaying the end.

A glare of lighting reflects across the wet world. My eyes flutter, and I nearly trip. I collect myself, only to hear the roots of a tree just feet behind me ripping from the earth like a weed. Branches pop as the tree crashes into the canyon wall.

How will he do it?

Drown me? Pierce me with his talon-like fingers? Crush me?

No, no. He looks too much like the riverwraiths—like he's the king of them. He'll probably thrash me against the trees and stones until my broken body releases my soul.

Another flare of lightning disorients my steps, and I trip just as his claw swipes for me. I faceplant into the mud, and his claw whooshes just over my head. He roars, reaching again, but I evade his grasp with a roll, not realizing where I am—on a slant. My body tumbles sideways and slides across the slimy grass until I crash into a tree. I tilt my head to see the monster scanning the ground for me, vortices still swirling around him. I pull myself up and bolt the opposite way. The sound of breaking trees follows directly after.

But as I run, a wild idea strikes me. *I can't kill him, but there is something that might.*

The lightning.

I just need to get him big enough to tower over the canyon walls.

I race toward the river, impressed with my own body's ability now that there's a freckle of hope. If I can just get him to the river, maybe he'll absorb it…

And the rest is up to chance.

I reach the gushing river and run alongside it, praying the beast isn't smart enough to know what I'm thinking. My ears open to the noises behind me. More snapping wood. A rumble from the beast that almost sounds like laughter. The gurgling hiss of disturbed water. *It's working. He's absorbing the river.* But I can't look back to watch him grow—his reach is expanding with every foot taller that he gets.

Please, Illuminant. Help me. I pray toward the sky. The lightning flashes, and I hope it's his answer, his power surging to my rescue.

Instead, a wet wave slams into my back, vaulting me forward. I crash face-first for the second time, but now, I feel the presence of the golem like a shadow falling over me. I spin to face him, knowing there is no escape. Whatever he's going to do, it's over.

The Illuminant didn't listen. *Why should he with this mark on my wrist?*

The monster's heathen eyes hone in on me and his giant claw opens. But then, in a blur of ivory, something comes between us. I blink my vision clear.

No!

"Vaeryn!" I shout just as the rock-hard backhand of the beast smashes into her, flinging her body like a doll until she thuds into the thick mud.

In the distance, I can't see her face or if she's breathing. *Is she dead? Unconscious?* She doesn't move at all. Everything seems to freeze around me, even the rain. Why did she come back? Why would she put herself between me and the beast when there's nothing she could do to stop him?

A sharp cry from above wrenches my focus away. Then I see it—wide, iridescent wings soaring across the sky, gathering the electricity. Bolts crackle over a bird's feathers and spark down its ribbon-like tail as it surges toward the monster.

Raphós?

My breath leaks out of my parted lips as the bird glides, carrying the lightning straight into the golem's core. Webs of electricity spider through the beast, illuminating his whole body. I shield my eyes from the brilliance until it fades, and when I look back, the monster has evaporated, even its shells. And Raphós is nowhere in sight.

He came. My breath catches. *The Illuminant did listen.*

For Vaeryn.

I stumble to her and drop, knees sinking into the sludge beside her. She blinks as my trembling hand lays against her shoulder. Then slowly, she rolls onto her back, groaning as her body resettles. The slowing rain trickles over her mud-splattered face and hair, gently washing it as she stares at me.

A dozen questions war for first behind my teeth, but none break out before she speaks.

"You're clever for a smith."

Her words tug at cords inside my chest—she said them to me back in Fenfyre. But this time they come out so weak, they feel like the last ones she might ever say.

"Where are you hurt?" I ask.

"My hip, mostly." She lays her hand on it, and I notice her arm is laced in blood. "That's where he struck me."

"Is it broken?"

"Let's find out. Help me sit, will you?"

I take her arm and cautiously pull her upright. Despite her restrained whine, she manages.

"Feels terrible." Her vocal cords sound pinched. "But I didn't feel anything shifting. Probably just a wretched bruise. Rather fortunate, considering."

"*Considering* you threw yourself between me and a giant nether-beast without any armor and no way to defend yourself," I say, hoping my eyes show my gratitude in spite of my rebuke.

"Not the wisest move," she says, lying back in the mud. "But what else could I do?"

"Forget about me and go through the portal like I told you to."

A soft chuckle puffs from her nose before her smile fades, and her expression turns void. "There is no forgetting."

The warmth fades in my chest. *Guilt.* That's why she came for me. She just couldn't handle the burden of knowing someone else died for her sake after what happened to Verik.

And for a moment, I thought I meant something real to her.

I turn away and wait for her to decide she's ready to move on. When she is, I help her up, only to find that she can hardly walk on her own.

Was it worth it? I want to ask. Instead, I offer my help again. She reluctantly accepts, and I put my arm under hers and wrap it around her. The feeling of her so close consumes me—her warmth permeating through her thin shirt, the shifting of her shoulder blades, the rising and falling of her back as she breathes. We've never been this close besides when she was unconscious. But that was different.

I still had hope then.

I lead her past all the broken trees. The monster that destroyed them already feels like something I faced hours ago. And the place we walk toward doesn't even feel real. As it shouldn't. Because I can already sense the portal's rejection. This mark staining my wrist will leave me standing here among the wreckage.

Alone.

I doubt Raphós would come back to help me home either.

"Our stuff," I say when we finally make it to where the lake once stood. All that's left are puddles and the stone arch portal, glowing like a watery window.

I help Vaeryn over to a tree so she can support herself against it while I gather everything.

"You putting any of this back on?" I ask, gesturing to her armor.

"Just my boots," she says. "I shouldn't need anything else."

I stuff her armor into her bag while she hobbles to a rock. The suppressed whine in her throat doesn't pass my notice as she sits. I straddle her boots between two fingers and bring them over, but only once I'm standing there do I realize how hard it would be for her to put them on herself. I resist a frown, bitterness strangling like thorns inside my chest.

Are we even friends? Or is everything that made it feel like we are for her own peace?

I kneel without saying anything and loosen the laces of her boot. When I lift the shoe, she makes no effort to raise her leg from the ground. I look up, biting my cheek in my frustration, but then I see the tears welling in her eyes. She blinks and one falls. Her hands never wipe it. She just leaves it to slip around her flushed cheeks and down the curve of her neck. The tear douses my frustration. Water to a wick.

I'm lucky to even be here, and I know it. I shouldn't expect anything more from her than basic courtesies. She's not my friend. She's the Illuminarch. Fooling myself into thinking there could ever be anything more was my mistake—one I'm not even sure when I let happen. I'm just a servant. A means of getting what she needs, just like I was to Father and Niah. As soon as she walks through that portal, she's going to forget me like they probably already have.

"I'm not ready to go through," she says, glancing toward the passage.

I hold the boot tighter. "Won't stay quiet around here for long."

"I know."

I lift her foot for her and awkwardly finagle the boot over it. When I look up again, another tear is trailing down her face.

"You're gonna be a great Illuminarch, Vaeryn."

"It's not that."

I grab the second boot. "Then what is it?"

I've shimmied that boot on and laced it up before she answers. "I'm worried that you're right."

"About?"

She stands, and I do the same. Her eyes weigh into mine, still dewy and lined in red. "The portal not letting you through."

I flinch. *What?*

"Ezro…if it doesn't…" Her face scrunches like she's fighting for the right words. "If it doesn't, I want you to know what you've done for me—protecting me all this way—it means more than I know how to tell you."

I swallow, a wall in my heart steadily assuring me this is just her guilty conscious speaking.

"Thank you," she says, stepping closer, even though it makes her wince. "For the arrows. For showing up right when I needed you the most, and offering your help even in the wake of your own losses. I could never repay you, but I swear upon my life to do everything I can to liberate this kingdom and bring justice on your mother's account. And I truly hope that if that mark keeps you from entering the Etherium, I can find you again as soon as I'm able."

My mind empties of all words, but she leaves no chance for me to speak anyway before she takes another step and wraps her arms around me. My body tenses, skin numbing at her embrace. Her arms squeeze tight enough to make me believe her words are true.

She's afraid to lose me. I matter to her. I matter.

To her.

The warmth returns inside my chest, and I hug her back. Something in me burns to say something in exchange. To tell her how long overdue I am for an embrace like this. Or how my soul seemed to seep from my body when she was pulled into the lake. Or to thank her for risking her life for mine. *Her life,* one that flows with the blood of Luminors in her veins. *For mine,* one whose family has served the netherworld in selfish allegiance for a century.

But I don't know how to say any of it. So I just hold her back, appreciating the way it all feels until she steps away and smiles at me.

"There. I think I'm ready now," she says.

But I feel less ready than I've ever been. If the portal rejects me, I'll have to walk through those tunnels alone, all the way out of the canyon. And then what? Where do I go? To Jarden? Back to my father so he can turn me in for execution?

No. How could I go back there? There's nothing for me. Anywhere. Anywhere but right here and through that portal.

Illuminant, please, I plead from within. *Let me pass through. Please let me through.*

"Are *you* ready?" Vaeryn asks.

"Never could be," I say, putting my arm around her to help her walk. "Let's go."

32

EZRO

When my foot passes through the iridescent pane of the portal, the terror of death surges through my nerves. I expect my foot to land and my heart to stop. Or for fire to consume me. Or lightning to strike me down like it had the water golem. Instead, my sole settles onto solid ground. And the other follows.

I hold my eyes shut, not wanting to see what judgment looks like as it hovers before me. But when the only harsh sensation that meets me is a bitter cold, I open my eyes, and they are drawn immediately to the glowing stones floating around us. They hang in the air as if by invisible strings, twinkling like multi-hued stars. Beyond them, crystalline mountains separate the black sky from the dark earth. Light refracts through the glass-like mounts, swathing the ground in shades of warm gold and teal. Overhead, vibrant colors flow across the starless sky like ribbons caught in the wind. I trace them to their source—a tall tower that stands like a lighthouse miles away, with a pillar of light piercing indefinitely into the sky.

There it is, I realize. *The Light of the Luminors. Just waiting for Vaeryn to reach it.*

I stare, captivated, for several moments before my gaze drags down the tower to the white-coated ground surrounding it. The vague formation of a castle-like building sits between here and the tower, its roof spotted with snow. The snow dissipates over the long stretch, but the chill penetrates through my skin and damp clothes.

Vaeryn's warmth against my side reminds me that she's still relying on me to stand. I turn my gaze to her, expecting to see her admiring the ethereal world around us, but her eyes are locked on me. A nearby mountain casts a teal light across her face. I swallow hard—she fits right into the beauty of this place, just as she should. How I'm still alive and standing here with her eludes me. But I am. And Vaeryn is looking at me as if the wonders surrounding us don't even exist.

"You made it," she whispers through a smile.

This far, I think to say, but I don't want to ruin this by reminding her of my uncertain fate if she attempts to anoint me. Besides, the Illuminant sent Raphós to defend her in the canyon. Maybe he'll spare me for *her* sake.

"I made it," I say instead, returning her smile.

I glance at my wrist, finding the crescent still there, but Vaeryn's relieved sigh blows my disappointment away. She rests her head against my shoulder—a feeling I could get used to—but it only lasts a few seconds before she straightens out and turns her focus on the building in the distance.

"That's the Luminors' sanctuary," she says. "We should rest there a few days, let this injury subside before traveling to the Light."

I nod.

We take a step forward and the levitating stones spin into motion, parting from our path on each side. They slowly resettle, lights of all different shades gently pulsing from their cores. My hands ache to reach for one and hold it, but I doubt the stones would let me. Maybe that's why they parted—so I wouldn't contaminate them if I were to brush into one.

Fern-like bushes appear along the path as we walk toward the snow-capped building. The plants' dark, iridescent leaves curl downward as we pass them, almost as if they were bowing. I glance at Vaeryn to ask about it, but then it hits me. *The Etherium isn't responding to me. It's responding to her. It knows the Illuminarch has arrived.*

My tension eases, and suddenly I'm not sure what's more amazing to me—this mesmerizing world, or the fact that I'm the one walking the future Illuminarch through it.

The air gets colder the farther we walk, and soon the snow I'd seen off in the distance is splattered across our path. The cold leaks through the soles of my boots as we step onto it, and I bite down to keep my teeth from chattering. Vaeryn holds me tighter, either for her rising nerves or sympathy, knowing I have no experience with weather this frigid. Whatever her reason, it makes my heart thrum. *Will this end?* I can't help but wonder. *Once she claims her power, will she become so consumed in her new role that she forgets what I mean to her?*

The thoughts dissolve as we near the towering building she called the sanctuary. At first, the stone walls are plain and unimpressive, but as we step into the courtyard, elegant, glowing whorls ignite on the walls. Then, over every window and door, tiny gems twinkle to life, like archways made of stars. Both our feet halt to admire the dazzling building before Vaeryn directs our steps to the door.

"There should be some warmer clothes inside. Drier at least," she says.

I bite back my laugh. "Always wanted to try on one hundred-year-old clothes."

"Nothing wears in the Etherium," she counters, missing the joke. "And Father said the sanctuary has a way of…resupplying itself. I wouldn't be so quick to discredit the blessings the Illuminant has placed over this realm. It was his gift to his most selfless servants."

"Does he keep the pantry stocked?" I tease as we reach the doorstep.

Vaeryn slips from my support and gives me something just shy of a glower, then she tugs on the heavy double door. It doesn't budge. She bites her lip, thinking for a moment before she speaks to the door in a foreign language. "*Emos thelómia, ani magami. Naphòs thelómia, ani abatreuó.*"

I open my mouth to ask what she said, but before a sound gets out, she's opening the door. She steps in first, and I stand outside, peering into the softly lit foyer. Around her, I see a radiant, shimmering floor and two wide staircases that lead in opposite directions. Between them, another double door separates the foyer from the rest of the sanctuary.

Vaeryn limps in, a faded legion of shadows sprouting under her feet from the multitude of light sources. She reaches the center of the foyer, just between the stairs, before she looks back and sees me standing outside.

"It's not going to kill you," she says. "Just come inside."

I'd like to ask how she knows, but I follow her orders and walk in. I reach her, still alive, and breathe my anxiety out again. She smiles and takes my arm. Then, pointing, she says, "Up there should be the Luminors' private chambers, if I remember my father's illustration of it right."

I nod and aid her up the stairs. She masks the pain of every step with a thin smile, and soon we are standing in a long corridor. We divide into separate rooms. The one I pick reminds me of the inn we stayed at in Rōsrun; except that it's cleaner and the elaborately carved bed posts make it look like a king is supposed to sleep here.

I plop my backpack onto the bed and tend first to the gash on my palm from when I fell. Once it's cleansed and bandaged, I swing the wardrobe door wide. I reach in only to realize that the rack is filled with dresses, ruffled blouses, and skirts. I scowl and shut the doors, turning to try the wardrobe in the next room instead.

It takes three tries to find clothes that will work, but when I do, it's like someone tailored the entire wardrobe just for me. I slip on a pair of trousers and a long-sleeved shirt that buttons at the collar. Then I find a long, hooded crimson coat with leather detailing. It's far more dramatic than anything I've ever thought about wearing, but it's warm, so I shove my arms through and button it up. I tighten all the buckles, sealing out the cold air, and look over at a full-length mirror. I almost laugh at my reflection. I *look* like a Luminor.

But stars know, I'll be dead as soon as I try to become one. I'm surprised the clothes aren't burning me.

I add my boots—the only things of mine that didn't get soaked by the rain—and march out. The hall is empty, but I hear shuffling in the farthest room down. I sit on the stairs, admiring the intricate designs in the metal handrail, until Vaeryn's door opens.

She emerges with her hair loose and wearing a white blouse that puffs around her wrists. The only added layers on her are a vest and a skirt that laces at her hips but then divides, revealing a fitted pair of pants and a fresh pair of knee-high boots. No armor. No coat. It's the closest she's ever looked to a regular woman that I might have run across in Fenfyre, besides her pale skin. But she's not regular. Not even slightly. And someday, maybe not long from now, I'll see her the way she's supposed to be. Crowned and draped in fine clothes, overlooking her kingdom.

Her brows raise when she sees me, a laugh she tries to cover with her hand following just after. Immediately, I regret adding this obnoxious coat. It would have been better to freeze than for her to laugh at me.

Her hand lowers once she's composed herself, but still, she says nothing.

"What?" I finally ask. "It was the only coat I could find."

She laughs again, this time, not bothering to hide it. "I'm sorry. Really, it's lovely…"

"Then why are you laughing?"

"It's nothing," she says. "Stand up. Let's see it."

Air huffs from my nose. I rise, freshly aware of my aching muscles after all that's happened today. Vaeryn inspects my choices from head to toe, fighting a smile the whole time. Despite the embarrassment heating my hands, I can't help but smile back. She seems so much different here already. Like the armor she's been wearing melted when we stepped into the Etherium, and now the real her is standing here. Young and vibrant, despite having nearly drowned a few hours ago.

"It suits you," she says. Her smile wavers with her every painful step as she walks over.

"How long did it take you to find all that?" I ask.

She looks down at herself. "One try. I am practically my great-grandmother's twin; I figured starting there was wise. It is odd, though, wearing clothes she once did."

I almost respond when I notice her neck is bare for the first time. She's left the pendant off. But what does that mean? That she's letting Verik go, or that she doesn't feel right wearing that crescent charm in this place?

The silence is just turning awkward when she looks back up and says, "Let's hope her crown fits me as well as her clothes. Now, let's go see about that pantry, shall we?"

33

VAERYN

THE COOL AIR EMBRACES ME WITH A FEELING OF HOME AS I SETTLE onto a bench on the balcony. The sky beyond the blue-green aurora is still black despite the arrival of morning. But it won't be like this much longer. Father once said the Etherium stays dark all hours of the day when there isn't an Illuminarch, but when one is anointed, the day and night cycles return to the sky.

I never imagined that the person who would restore that cycle would be me.

I look at the Light spearing through the darkness in the distance. As soon as I've recovered enough, I will be standing before it, accepting a future that should never have been mine. In the face of it, I'm not sure I want it at all. I would have much preferred Father had set out before his injury or that Liander hadn't cowered from it. Instead, I must carry this burden to start and win this war against the netherworld. But I won't be like Liander. No matter the fear, the doubt, the heaviness, I won't leave these innocent people to suffer for my own comfort.

Solalé's reign must end. The beasts must be ridden of. And if I must be the one to make that happen, then so be it.

I retrieve my pendant from the pocket I hid it in and rub my thumb along the slick moonstone. The crescent charm glints under the aurora, an ironic sight.

And a painful one. Verik was supposed to be here with me, but now, all I can do is dread what would have happened if he was. Would he be forcing me on right now? Offering me no chance to recover? Or would he gladly leave me here while he went alone, to attempt to claim the Light for himself?

The latter, I realize, is the most likely. And he'd sweetly chalk it up to sparing me of the pain and responsibility.

I sigh, readjusting my position to take the weight off the deep bruise on my hip. Even knowing how terrible Verik's presence here would be, my bones still ache at the thought of him. How could anyone be so selfish?

A tear just slips onto my cheek when Ezro's voice lurches my shoulders. "You trying to be alone?"

"Not necessarily. Just thinking." I clutch the pendant as his steps draw closer, but not quickly enough to conceal it.

"You don't have to keep hiding that thing," he says.

I tuck it away despite and wipe my face dry before looking at him. He's wearing that crimson coat he found yesterday, the hood pulled up to keep the cold off his ears. Still, his hair finds a way to fall onto his forehead. He looks at the bench as if to ask if he can sit. I nod, and he fills the empty space beside me.

"It must be hard not to think about him here," he says, resting his folded hands on his knees.

I hold my tongue, debating if I'll engage in this conversation or shut it down. Why he bothers with it, I don't understand. Have I misread the longing in his eyes for something deeper between us? Or is he so kind that he'd choose to suffer the pain of listening to me talk about some past love of mine just to further prove to me he deserves to be the next?

"You're right about him," I say. "I know you are. I never told you that."

His lips thin, sealing in his silence.

"I also never thanked you for risking being honest with me."

"Yeah, thought for sure I'd end up beneath your boot again," he teases, but his tone turns serious. "Still not sure if I made it better for you or worse."

I stare at the tranquil glow of the mountains. "That's the thing. I'm not sure which is worse. To have something real die prematurely, or have the whole thing be a lie. But at least I know what to let go of now, and why it was so hard before." I let out a breath and return my gaze to his. The warmth of his eyes melts a layer of my sorrow away, but it's so thick, there is no telling if I'll ever be fully rid of it. Still, I press on a smile and propose a change of topic. "I wish you could see how good of a person you are."

A somber chuckle draws a weak smile onto his lips, but he looks away.

"I mean it," I press. "I'd never have made it here without you. I'd have turned back, probably died on the way home. And if not in flesh, then in spirit. I owe you more than I think I can repay for all you've done for me."

"I wanted to do it. You don't owe me for that," he says. "The kingdom needs you, anyway."

"You will let me anoint you, won't you? You said you'd decide if you made it in here, and here you are."

His chin tucks toward his chest. "I'm still not convinced the Illuminant will have me as a Luminor. Might be the last you see of me if you try."

"That mark"—I thoughtlessly grab his wrist and turn it up to show the crescent—"is nothing more than a stain on your wrist. You've seen what it can do to other people. In what way has this ever corrupted your actions or words?"

He's quiet, eyes fixed on my hand that's holding his wrist. I should let go, but I want his answer first. But it never comes, and in his silence, my point is proven.

I keep my hand where it is. "The mark cannot corrupt one of the Illuminant's Faithful. That is what I've come to believe after what you taught me. And you may well be more faithful to the Illuminant in character than even myself. So, forget about this mark." I turn his wrist around and tug his sleeve to further hide it. "And tell me you will accept the anointing because I can't do this without you."

"Can't or don't want to?"

"Both."

His half-hearted smile returns but his eyes feel heavier when he looks at me again. "Vaeryn, I'd follow you anywhere."

"Why?" I regret the question as soon as it's out.

He gives me a tired look and then laughs, averting his eyes. "Because you're the first person since my mother died who has ever looked at me and actually seen someone standing there." He allows me only a few seconds to absorb the stinging caress of his answer before he stands and throws on a familiar smirk. "And you're worth following, Vaeryn. Never met anyone half as brave or noble as you."

"Only because you haven't met yourself."

He straightens his crimson hood and shakes his head.

"You're going to make a great Luminor," I say before he can walk off.

"I'll try to be," he says, a cloud puffing from his lips as he sighs into the cold. "I'm going back in. It's freezing out here. Need any-thing?"

My lips part to decline, but then, like a firefly lighting up in my mind, I realize there is something after all. "You haven't seen any empty journals about, have you?"

"Yours full?"

"Filled it days ago."

"And you're still alive?" he teases, gripping his hood like it might fly back from the shock.

I try to grimace, but my smile plays it soft. "Barely."

He studies me, same as he always does when I joke back, like he didn't realize I had a sense of humor at all. Then his floppy smile returns. "I'll take a look in that study. Been wanting to rummage in there anyway."

"I'll look," I say. "I was just checking if you'd noticed one."

His eyelids droop to a half-lidded stare. "You're injured. And I'm bored. Don't even think about it."

I bite my lip, now curious myself about what lies in that study. "Well, at least let me join you. There's a chaise in there."

He shrugs and returns to me with an outstretched hand.

34

EZRO

Nearly a week passes before Vaeryn says, "I'm ready" at what would be noon if the sun touched this place.

Her words strike me from across the common room where we've sat in silence, staring at the everlasting flames in the fireplace, and I sit up straight.

"Right now?" I ask.

Vaeryn's eyes remain fixed on the blaze. "Before I lose the nerve."

She inhales and stands, walking with no aid, as if to prove her recovery. I know it's not total. The bruise on her hip is probably only halfway healed and the rest is her stubborn tenacity. She pulls a long jacket off the coat rack, another of her great-grandmother's items, and starts buttoning it from the top down. My crimson coat is thrust into my face right as I'm standing. We both laugh at the accident—or what I *think* was an accident—before the seriousness of what we're dressing for flattens both our faces.

This is it. This is the day Vaeryn becomes the Illuminarch.

And somehow, I doubt any dark being from Paran'dan to the Netherworld will go without noticing it. Solalé, especially.

We're striking a match and tossing it straight into the brush. Soon all hell will be upon us, just waiting for us to step outside.

I shove my feet into my boots, the thick wool socks forcing me to loosen the laces. But it's a long walk in the snow from here, and so far, I've barely withstood twenty minutes outside without shivering.

The cold bites my exposed face as we step out. I pat my hood against my ears to block the nippy breeze and rub my partially gloved hands together. Vaeryn, layered only by her coat, looks out at the light-laced sky. A wintry wind sighs between us, and brilliant strands slip loose from her freshly tied braid. It reminds me of being in the canyon. On a mission.

I should have known she was ready just by the fact she came out with her hair braided instead of loose like she's worn it since we arrived.

She's the first to take a step into the snow, and though she holds her head high, just a glance in her eyes gives away her anxiety.

"Just focus on this," I say. "Don't worry about everything that comes after. Today should be a good day for you, a day to celebrate."

She keeps her eyes set on the tower a far stretch ahead of us. "I wish I was more excited."

"What do you mean?"

Our synced footsteps crunch a dozen times before she answers. "I shouldn't talk about it."

"Maybe you should?"

An array of floating rocks sway from our path like fleeing birds.

Vaeryn sighs a white cloud, looking at me with eyes that seem as worn as they are grateful. "When I was a child, I believed my father would walk these steps. I thought he'd save the entire kingdom, then someday, hand it to my brother, since he's the eldest. I never thought the role would become mine. Even when I set out for it, I didn't expect that I'd *make it*." Her chin lowers. "I suppose a part of me wishes Liander hadn't cowered from this. Left it up to me."

"And you'd really be happy in your brother's shadow?" I ask.

"Happier, actually."

I raise a brow. "Really?"

"I'm shyer than you probably realize." She fiddles with a button of her coat, and it stirs memories of all the other times I've watched her fidget and flush. "So, yes, it never bothered me to think of my brother taking all the glory while I sat at a safe distance from the attention, doing what I could to help. Not everyone can be in center focus, and not everyone is made for it either. But alas, I'll adjust, I suppose. Clearly, this is the way the Illuminant must want it if I've made it here. *Emos thelómia, ani magami. Naphòs thelómia, ani abatreuó.*"

"What does that even mean?"

"It's the Luminors' mantra," she says like I should have known. "'My will, I surrender. The Iluminant's will, I serve.' It's Etherical. My father taught me much of the language, but that was the line he told me never to forget."

"Maybe he knew you'd be the one here."

She considers this longer than I expect before nodding. "Perhaps he did."

"I need to rest."

I stop mid-step, unclenching my jaw. I've been fighting not to say the same thing for the last mile with the way Vaeryn's been limping. I nod and help her lower into the snow. She scrapes the white powder, stacking it against her hip to ice it. Then she leans back with both hands pressed into the snow behind her to stare into the sky.

The aurora illuminates her face as it dances above. Why the Light doesn't anoint her from here and spare her the walk, I don't understand.

I pace back and forth a couple of steps before plopping across from her. The cold, wet ground presses against my thighs and the shiver I've been fighting finally wracks my body.

Vaeryn laughs, the last sound I expected for how stoic she's become after our last conversation.

"Remind me never to take you to Brïsbrook," she says.

"Is it colder than this?"

"Much."

She shuts her eyes like she's picturing it, a smile spreading across her face. I wonder if she's imagining us being there together, or if she's just wishing she never left. She sits like this for several long minutes, then her eyes snap open and her smile falls.

"I've been unfair to you," she says. "And only just now did I notice."

"How?" I ask.

"Do you *want* to be a Luminor, Ezro? Or are you only accepting it because I said I needed you?"

I jolt. "What kind of question is that?"

"One worth asking. I shouldn't have pressured you—"

"Yes," I cut in before she can ramble off about it. "I want to be a Luminor."

"But why? And don't say anything about me."

I look down to my hands. My fingertips—discolored by the cold—poke out beyond my gloves. I curl them in. "Because I'm tired of seeing darkness cover the light."

Vaeryn soaks in my answer a moment before she nods and reaches a hand toward me. I stare at it, confused at what she wants until she glances at one of my balled fists. I take her hand and pull us both to our feet, but she doesn't let go once stable. And there we stand, staring into each other's eyes, exchanging a silent encouragement for the final stretch to the tower.

"I'm glad it's you here with me," she says at last.

"Me too."

I glance at her smile, for the first time sensing it's okay to wonder what her lips feel like, but the Light shining in my peripheral stops me. *Not now.*

I turn, wrapping an arm around her to help her the rest of the way, and we walk.

35

VAERYN

A LOUD WHISTLE FILLS THE AIR AS WE DRAW NEAR THE TOWER, AND only once I squint do I realize where it's coming from. There's a wind wrapping around the labradorite tower in a tornado-like current, churning the flurries of snow. Yet, everywhere else, the land is still.

Ezro glances at me, seeming to notice the oddity of it at the same time.

"Perhaps it's a protection to keep those not of the Illuminarch's bloodline from going up," I say, though Father never mentioned anything like it. I don't see why else it would be there.

Ezro nods, accepting my response as a worthy reason. I push our steps quicker despite my pain. The snow crunches beneath our boots, its depth increasing unnaturally fast the farther we go. As we near it, the cold seems to reach to my very soul. *Where are the stairs? The ladder? The means to the top?*

We circle the massive stone tower, scanning the bumpy stone surface for any indication of a way up—or *in*, perhaps. But after two circuits, I find nothing. Not even an inscription to explain it. My burning nostrils flare.

"How am I supposed to get to it?" My voice cracks, and I break again from Ezro's support, only for my hip to cripple my step. I fall into the icy bed but feel none of its cold. All I feel is a fiery rage sweltering my skin.

Why aren't there stairs?

My hands crush the snow, mind digging for answers through everything my father has ever taught me. I shake my head, tears burning my eyes.

"You mentioned the canyon was a rite of passage," Ezro says over the wailing wind. "Maybe there's more to it?"

His suggestion seems to open a locked section of my memory. "A trial," I whisper, but my voice gains confidence as I speak. "Yes. Father did say the Light reappears in different places within the Etherium each time—somewhere different for each Illuminarch, but he wasn't sure why. Perhaps that's it. A final test. To be sure they are worthy."

I push myself to stand, but a sharp pang in my hip sends me back to the snowy ground. My gaze crawls over the incredible height of the tower, a tight grimace stretching my tense skin.

Could I even reach it if I wasn't injured? Could anyone?

I fumble another step closer before Ezro is beside me again, pulling me upright.

"I have to try to climb it," I say.

His brows cave. "Now?"

I nod, and his eyes bulge.

"You're injured, Vaeryn. If you're gonna try climbing that thing, you aren't doing it right now. You need to finish healing first."

I ball my hands, fighting an urge to shove him and his reasoning off. "Netherbeasts could be destroying a town right now. The kingdom's waited long enough."

His sights turn toward the tower. "Vaeryn, I have a lot of experience climbing. You're not getting up there. Not in the shape you're in."

A huff billows white from my mouth. "This could take weeks to fully heal, if not longer. And my anointing is only the beginning of a long journey before I can rise against Solalé and her beasts." I sound insane and I know it, but the rising panic in me won't be silenced. "It *cannot* wait. I *have* to at least try. The pain can be pushed through. It has to be. I've climbed plenty myself…"

I push him from me and force stability into my strides as I plow toward the tower. Every rotation of my hip stabs like a venomous fang.

"Vaeryn! Hold on!" Ezro shouts. "Just wait a second."

I whirl back to argue, but then I see his expression has softened, despite the obvious plea in his eyes for me to stop.

"Just be careful."

I swallow, offering a curt nod before turning. My teeth grit as I wade through the snow, setting my eyes on my first handhold. The violent wind roars into my ears and threatens my balance, but I sink my fingers between the bricks and pull myself onto the wall. My left side quivers as I force it to hold my weight. I restrain my groan and pull to my next grip, pain wrenching tears into my eyes. But when I reach for the next, the wind hits me like a wave. My balance falls onto my left side, and the shock of pain overtakes my body. My grip fails, and I topple, back slamming into the snow. The air is punched from my lungs, and all I can do is stare at the colorful lights streaming across the sky, cursing the distance between me and them.

I'm just shifting to rise when the outcry of a bird stills me. I search the sky until I spy his long, glistening feathers.

"Raphós," I whisper as his luminous wings swoop into view.

He cries out again, his ethereal voice more beautiful than any instrument man could invent and incomparable to any bird in our mortal world.

For a moment, my hopes lift, expecting him to whirl around the tower and perform a miraculous appearance of stairs. But he passes the tower, gliding toward us instead.

Has he come to heal me?

The question barely crosses my mind before Raphós passes me, too. I sit, spinning to watch as he flies toward Ezro. He circles him twice, then soars to the top of the tower where the Light awaits. With a final cry, he circles the Light and disappears into the sky.

My jaw falls, chest tingling. *What does he mean?*

But it's so obvious, I don't know why I bothered to ask myself.

"He wants you, Ezro," I say. "The Illuminant has chosen you instead."

36

EZRO

"He wants me to take you up there," I say, just as Vaeryn is speaking.

We both quiet, replaying to ourselves what the other said.

"If he wanted you to take me up there, he'd have circled me after you," she says before I can process her ridiculous claim. "He's signaling for *you*. You're the one the Illuminant wants. Not me."

My feet stagger back, almost tripping on the snow.

"*No*. He didn't circle you because there's no need. You're the heiress," I sputter, hands raised as if to block her words from getting any closer to me. "Why would the Illuminant choose me instead? He just wants me to get you up there. That's all he's saying."

"Ezro, that's not—"

"I could do it," I cut in, eyes turning back to the tower. "I could find a way to get you up there. Maybe we can find a rope somewhere in the sanctuary, bring it back here. I could go first and pull you up. We could even *make* a rope if there's nothing long enough. It would be hard because of the wind but—"

"*Stop*." Vaeryn is back on her feet when I face her again. She trudges through the snow until she's standing a reach away. "*I* am not the one the Illuminant has chosen. *You* are."

"I'm not the *heir*." I pull my sleeve back, holding up the crescent on my wrist. "And I'm—"

She knocks my hand down and my words go with it. "The Illuminant decided who you would be before anyone ever put that mark on you. You cannot keep—"

"Vaeryn, I'm *not* the heir!"

"Says who? *Who* decides who the Light belongs to?"

"Your ancestors have been the Illuminarchs for all generations," I say, head shaking. "The Illuminant isn't suddenly going to break that line just for me. It's *yours*. It belongs to you. To your family. I'm not going up there to take what's yours just because some bird flew around me."

"That *bird* is the spirit who has trained and counseled every Illuminarch since creation." Vaeryn's tone sharpens. "He *knows* the will of the Illuminant. And his will is *obvious*. You are the one he beckoned."

My fists ball. "Yeah, to help you. He doesn't want me to be the Illuminarch. He can't—"

She steps so close, her breath tickles my nose when she speaks. "What was I just telling you the other day? You are the truest person I've ever met. More faithful to the Illuminant in character than even myself. *Me*, the heir. *You*, the one marked and abused and deprived of every good thing. Who better to face the darkness in this kingdom than the one who has already endured it? Who better to lead the people back to the Illuminant than the one who never lost his faith, even when every trace of the Illuminant seemed missing? And what did I say that time you pushed us onward when I wanted to turn back? *It's like you were born for this.* And I've thought that a hundred more times than I've said."

She grabs my wrists, squeezing them as tears escape the corners of her eyes. "I know your heart yearns for this—for the power to change things. Try to tell me you don't want this. Try to convince me you don't long to be the one to lead this kingdom back to the Light, because I've never seen anyone more committed to it than you."

My skin numbs where her grip is. "If it was my mantle to take, I'd be climbing already. But it's not, and I'm not taking this from you, Vaeryn. That mantle is yours."

"You can't take from me what was never mine. It has always been yours. That's why my father's plan was thwarted. Why my brother cowered. Why Verik died so I would have no choice but to rely on you—it's all so *you* can be here. Can't you see it? *Can't you?*" Her hands slip from my wrists, only to grab my face and force me into her gaze. "It's yours. And I want you to have it. *Please*. Please, take it."

"Vaeryn—"

Her lips press into mine, dissolving my words, my doubts. All my senses flee besides a feeling of home deeper than I've ever known, as if our souls touched when our lips met and found the place they've always belonged. *Together.*

But it lasts for mere seconds before she pulls us apart and finds my bewildered eyes again. "This is who you are," she says, tears slipping into her smile. "Not that mark. Not what your grandfather did to you or what family you come from. *This* is who the Illuminant says you are."

My breath jerks, and suddenly, I notice the burning in my own eyes. *This can't be real. None of it. It can't be.* Why would the Illuminant choose me for this? Why, when Vaeryn is right here?

"You said you'd do anything to see an Illuminarch return. Why not this?" Vaeryn says, her thumbs wiping tears I never meant to weep, even as her own pour down her neck. "*Why not this?*" The second time she asks, it's a whisper, yet it feels louder than before. The conviction tugs me into silence.

My eyes squeeze shut, and suddenly I'm a child, with my mother's hands around my face. She's praying over me, the same words she said every night. *Lead him to the Light. Use him. Please use him.*

Did she know? *How could she know?*

My body is shaking. Cold and afraid. What if it's true? What if everything Vaeryn said is true? How could I withhold myself when a whole kingdom could be counting on me?

The thought opens my eyes, and I meet Vaeryn's face again. She's never looked more surreal to me than she does here, after that kiss. Standing here crying and pleading for me to do what she's said. I finally nod, and her sigh swirls between us in the cold. Her hands slip from my face as the mist dissipates. I want to ask her how she could do this—how she could stand there, convincing me to take what she's traveled so far for. But I can't muster a sound from my lips.

She steps out of my path, and my eyes set on the tower. I shed my tight coat, dropping it into the snow. Wind thrashes my hair as I approach it, every step closer, raising my pulse. I told Vaeryn I could climb it—a desperately overconfident claim—and now I'm not sure if I'll even reach the top to find out the truth. Or maybe that's the point. Maybe this is how the Illuminant judges me, by throwing me down with the Light far from reach. A final reminder that I have no place near anything holy.

My toes stop at the base of the tower, and I reach to grip my first handhold.

The wind ceases as my fingertips brush the stone.

37

EZRO

My chapped skin cracks, beads of blood forming over my knuckles. From far below, Vaeryn hollers, and I faintly catch her saying I'm halfway there. I don't look down. To fall is death, or close enough to death to prefer it.

My cramping hands pull me higher, numb to the touch yet aching in the bones. Every breath feels like it's cutting the back of my throat. I'd never have made it this high with the winds. Not even close. Even without them, I'm foolish to think I have any chance with how quickly my strength is sapping.

But the Illuminant called me.

I cling to that with everything, even as doubt tugs at my heels. Its weight is heavy, its accusations familiar. *You don't deserve this. You failed your family. You're stained with nethermagic. He only wants to judge you.*

"Then let him," I whisper, silencing the voice.

Below me, Vaeryn's shouts of encouragement fade into the distance as I climb, hand over hand, higher and higher. My muscles quiver in the effort of every motion, and the thinning air works a bleed from my nose that I can't wipe. The warm drip sinks into my mouth and taints my tongue with a metallic taste that reminds me too much of Grandfather's smithy. But I'm farther from him than I've ever been. What will he do when I come back as the Illuminarch?

I hope he falls on his knees in repentance to the Illuminant.

Father and Niah, too.

When I reach the final third, the stone slickens. My balance wavers, and I'm just barely able to catch myself to stop a fall. I still, realizing ice, too dark to be seen from the ground, has coated the last stretch to the top.

Ice. The one thing I know absolutely nothing about.

I clench the panic inside me. There's no downclimbing this. No backing out. The only path is up, but I'm shaking as I realize *up* might be a fast way *down.*

My hand grazes uncertainly across the slick surface. I grab the surest thing I find, digging my nails into it. I expect it to break when I pull up, but it stays. Sturdy as stone. I hoist up until every touch point I have is dependent on my natural nemesis, and the edge of the tower is within view.

Almost. I can do this.

I reach again with too much confidence and a jut of ice snaps off the wall. I jolt to recover my balance, but my foot slips, and suddenly I'm sliding down the tower. I yelp, fumbling for the knife in my belt with one hand, trying to catch myself with the other, but everything is too slippery to grasp. Finally, I get my knife loose and stab it into the ice with all my might. The blade holds just well enough for me to find footing and steady myself, though I don't think my heart will recover for the next ten years. I snag my second knife and stick it into the ice. With a jittery breath, I begin recouping the ground from my fall.

My arms shake as I reach the place where I'd slipped. The effort of yanking the knives out and thrusting them back into the ice increases in agony as I push through it again and again, until I don't know if my muscles bear the strength for this final stretch.

I play memories in my head like songs to distract me from the pain as I go. Distant memories of Mother and I playing in the cornfield, a summer sun splashing us through the stalks. Her laughter fills my ears and fades into a new sound: Vaeryn, telling me about Brïsbrook—of bonfires and warm clothes. Her voice is the most beautiful sound I've ever heard. I feel her hands on my face, her lips on mine— a new memory. Then I watch her tears slipping across her cheeks as she speaks her destiny over me as my own. *Life.* That is what she's sown in me. Life—when everything else was withering around me.

And what I would give to come down from this tower, the person that could fix this world for her. What future would we have if I make it? If we win?

I start playing it out, thoughts I've never once felt safe enough to consider, but soon I realize every one embodies a life that isn't mine. My thoughts are of us in Rōsrun, living a quiet, normal life in the little river town. And I'm ascending the tower to claim the Light—to claim the destiny of an Illuminarch.

My imagination can't fathom it. When it was her, it was so easy to see the crown on her head and royal robes across her shoulders.

But now it's me.

What do I know of running a kingdom? Of saving it?

Why? My thought directs to the sky. *Why would you pick me?*

But the question turns dim as a star in daylight when my knives sink into the rim of the tower. I struggle to get myself onto the base, fumbling onto the paved floor like a dead man. And there I lay, staring at the luminance, all the shades I couldn't see from afar. All the power I couldn't feel, tingling against my skin. Vapor clouds from my mouth, glimmering in the luster as it dissipates and reforms, and I don't know what to do with it—with my breath. How dare I even breathe in the presence of the Illuminant's Light?

He called me.

I don't know how many times I have to say it to myself for me to believe it. Maybe I never will, but that won't change the truth.

My weak arms push me upright, and I crawl in exhaustion to the silver pedestal the Light radiates from. I drop there on my knees, words creeping from my weary soul.

"Use me."

The request hangs in a quiet so deep that I wonder if the Illuminant has stolen my hearing as punishment for coming here. I sit in it, sinking further into doubt with each silent second that passes. My warm blood pulses through my veins—throbbing hardest where the bronze crescent stains my skin, reminding me of who I am and who I'm not.

Not an heir. Not even of pure heritage.

Just a means to an end.

Then suddenly, a crackle breaks the quiet, like the earsplitting pop of lightning, and a light as brilliant as an exploding sun erupts inside my mind.

And then it comes. The blackness I expected. And my thoughts fade into it like smoke.

38

EZRO

I awaken with a gasp like I've come up from underwater. My eyes open wide to the sight of trees. A vague light from below glints on the fire-toned leaves that cover me like a canopy, so dense I can barely see the pitch-black sky behind them. *Where am I?* I stroke the ground, rubbery grass running through my fingers. A rich breeze rushes across my tingling skin as I sit. Trees surround me in every direction, swarming the landscape until they are lost in the darkness.

How did I get here? Where was I before I fell asleep?

My eyes stop on a glowing dandelion, trembling in the grass. A fuzzy seed breaks loose and catches in the wind like a winter flurry. *Snow. Wasn't I just in snow?* I watch the seed fly until it catches in the grass, wringing my memory to recall where I last was. *What was I doing? What landed me here?*

And then it hits me like a splash of ice water to the face. The Light. The tower. The explosion in my mind. The darkness…

But what happened? I was beckoned up there to be anointed, but then why do I feel no different? Wouldn't I know if the power of the Illuminarch had entered me?

212

What am I doing here?

I stand, slowly pivoting. This couldn't still be the Etherium, could it? Did the Illuminant just transport me away from the Light? Was this his mercy for us mistaking who he wanted? To cast me off instead of killing me for it?

Where is Vaeryn?

I holler her name, running a few paces in a random direction, but nothing answers except the breeze fluttering the leaves. My body stills. I turn around again, as if someone might emerge from the trees to explain this all to me. But I'm alone for as far as I can see. Just me and trees as tall as hills. I reach for the trunk of the nearest one, thinking I might climb it to look for the sanctuary, but just as my fingers touch the bark, I feel a stir in my chest strong enough that I pull my hand away and twist in a different direction.

Go deeper, the urge tells me. And I can't resist it.

Crisp leaves crunch like dry desert ground beneath my soles. I walk for what feels like miles, weaving through the trunks, dodging low-hanging branches and luminescent boulders. The luring grows stronger the longer I follow it, until I can feel it pulsing in my hands like a second heartbeat.

My breaths start to shallow as I draw closer, until I know I'm going to stumble upon it at any moment. Like the mist you feel just before stepping from under an awning into the rain. It's there. So close. Just a reach away—

A tree?

My hand is stretching toward the gray trunk before I even realized I'd raised it. But that can't be it. Why a tree? There must be hundreds of trees in here—

But as I turn away, a sudden glimmer catches my attention. I still, watching as glowing golden whorls paint themselves onto the bark. I recognize the pattern immediately—I've stared at it on pages all my life.

The swirls spread until they cover every branch, pulsing with the same energy I'd felt from afar. And now, as if someone whispered it to me, I understand. The tower *was* a test. But this—*this* is where the Light is. In a tree—much like the oak I'd surrendered my past to. And here stands another tree, offering me the future the Illuminant traded my history for.

My future as an Illuminarch.

I stare at the tree until it hurts to keep my hand away. The kingdom has suffered for a century. Who am I to make that any longer?

I lay my palm against the warm bark and a surge of energy shoots down my arms and into my core. My mind fills with cascading images, replaying all the memories that got me here from the moment Vaeryn walked into the smithy to the moment we stepped through the portal. But the visions slow on one final image: me, kneeling beneath the Light.

"Use me," I hear myself utter, my mother's voice whispering beneath it, *Use him. Lead him to the Light.*

My eyes open to a golden light radiating on my arms. I gawk at the elaborate whorls as their glow is slowly doused, leaving behind pale markings on my skin that hide all the scars my grandfather gave me. The tingle of energy fades with it and settles inside my center, until it's little more than a flutter, like a moth trapped in my ribcage. I run a hand across the white marks.

The marks of an Illuminarch.

I fall, weeping, to my knees.

39

EZRO

Light floods the sky, filtering like sun rays through the fire-toned trees. My head lifts, bleary from the long weep on my knees, and for a minute, all I can do is stare at the vibrant sky—lit again after one hundred years of darkness.

For me.

My legs quiver as I rise and look through the endless sprawl of trees. Which way leads back to the tower? *To Vaeryn?*

My heart stutters recalling how I'd left her—crippled in the snow while I took her mantle. Her power. Her purpose. All the tension the Light had soothed from my body comes rushing back, like its peace was a mere illusion. *What have I done to Vaeryn?*

My gaze falls back to the markings on my arms. *Will the sight of them stir regret in her? Remorse for me being chosen? Or did she really mean what she said about wanting me to have this?*

I start walking, unsure where I'm going. My steps swerve between the many trees, unsteady. But I hardly get anywhere before a chirp swivels me around. I search between the vibrant branches until I catch the glisten of a bird's tail. *Raphós.* He swoops past me and dives downward. A brilliant light erupts when he collides with the ground, dazzling my eyes. I blink my vision clear to find a cloaked figure standing in the bird's place. His elaborate hood shadows his blue-tinged face, but even in the shade, his cerulean eyes gleam like portals to another world.

"Your feet and your heart are going in opposite directions," he says, his ethereal voice in my ears and mind at the same time.

I glance back the way I was headed. *Isn't that the way back to the tower?*

He smiles, then strides toward me, his navy cloak billowing as if caught in a wind though the air is still. I slip a step back before I can remind myself what he is: the spirit of the Etherium—not something of the netherworld.

He stops, near enough for me to notice the faint markings decorating his face before his fingers suddenly press my forehead. I flinch, eyes slamming shut as a sensation of falling rattles my pulse. It lasts only a second before a different feeling wraps over my skin. *Stillness. Warmth.*

I open my eyes and find I'm standing in the sanctuary, just beyond the common room. Heavy breaths wrack my body, mind fumbling to process what just happened. Raphós *transported* me here. *By a single touch.*

Where was *that* in the canyon?

The irritation the thought breeds shrivels when I register a soft noise in the common room. My eyes hone on the backside of the tall, leather couch. *Breathing.*

Vaeryn.

My boots pad the glossy floor until I step onto the thick rug. I quietly peer over the couch and find her beneath a wool blanket, asleep. *How long have I been gone?* I take a silent step closer, noticing tears shining on her cheeks and the purple-red splotches around her eyes—the face of someone who cried themself to sleep.

My shoulders slump, guilt crawling across my skin in the shape of these marks.

She said this is what she wanted, I tell myself to banish the guilt. *But why is she crying then?*

A lump builds in my throat.

I push myself toward her and kneel beside the couch. Without forethought, I push a tear-sopped strand of hair away from her eyes. My fingers graze her cool skin, and I expect her to wake. She doesn't. I try it again, brushing a phantom strand. This time, her face softens, but her eyes remain shut.

My gaze lowers to her gently parted lips, remembering how they'd silenced me at the tower. The thought of kissing them now, to see if that wakes her, crosses my mind and falls into a pit. *No.* Not now. Maybe not ever again when she sees these marks…

My posture wilts, but I draw in a steady breath.

"Vaeryn," I whisper.

Her brows scrunch, but her eyes remain sealed.

"I'm here," I say, stroking a fresh tear from her cheek.

She gasps, eyes opening wide enough for me to see my reflection in her pupils. The soft smile on my lips masks the nerves sparking through my system as her gaze shifts to the white swirls on my arms.

"I'm here," I repeat.

She releases a sharp cry and, suddenly, her arms are wrapped around my neck. "I thought you were dead," she whimpers. Then she's crying—crying and laughing at once. Her embrace tightens until I can hardly breathe. I hold her back, leaning my head against hers, and relish in the sounds of her relief until they settle.

She peels herself away, lips flickering like she wants to say everything and nothing at once. Another tear streaks her cheek, but her smile remains. Warmth kindles in my bones. She didn't strike me as a crier when we first met, but I like this better—her heart pouring out where I can see it.

And it's so beautiful. So kind, so selfless—unlike anyone I've ever known since Mother.

She sniffles, attention abruptly shifting to the room around us like it's the first time she's noticed where she is. "Did you…carry me here?"

Tightness eases from my chest as it dawns on me. "It was Raphós. He brought you here."

She processes my response slowly before dabbing her face dry with the blanket. "I don't remember it. I must've…fallen unconscious at the tower."

My thumb twitches. *When she thought me dead.*

"What did you see?" I ask.

She leans her back against the couch, chest swelling with her deep inhale. "The Light flashed, then disappeared from the sky. I couldn't see to the top of the tower, but I called out for you for ages, it felt like. When you never answered, I…" Her eyes avert me, focusing on a window now shining with daylight. "I feared you were right after all, that the Illuminant had judged you for that mark." Her brows scrunch, and she reaches for my hand. "Is it—?"

I give it to her and let her turn my wrist to see.

"It is," she says, smiling at the bronze crescent's absence.

"You were right, Vaeryn. About everything," I say. "Besides me being dead. I *think*."

She chuckles, hand recoiling to dab her tears again. I admire her calm expression, until the sight of it stirs a nervous tickle in my chest.

"Are you mad? About what happened?" I ask, gaze reaching into hers. "*Honestly.*"

Her chin lowers, and with it, her smile. "How could I be? I thought you dead and hope lost when last I was awake." Her hands squeeze the rim of her blanket as she meets my eyes again. "This is confusing, yes. But not angering. Not when it's you. Not when it's the Illuminant's will."

I search her eyes for lies—she's so good at them, after all—but I can't detect them.

Her smile creeps back, and she touches my chin with her fingers. "Besides, it's high time someone else looked at you and saw someone standing there."

Her words—or *my words*, repeated on her lips—weave right between my ribs and into my heart.

"I was satisfied when it was only you," I say.

"Stay that way, and you'll do just fine." She laughs, heavier than before, and her fingers slip from my chin. "If anything worries me about all this, it's *that*. Power and responsibility has a way of changing people, and I don't think I'd like that much."

"If I changed?"

She nods, and my teeth clench. I've had this conversation before—with Niah, under a different context and about a very different type of mark.

I lean closer so she can't miss the sincerity in my eyes.

"Nothing's going to change me, Vaeryn," I say. "I promise."

EPILOGUE

Sunlight refracts through the wall-length windows of the royal court. Shards of colorful light speckle across the polished moonstone floor and glint on the bronze armor of Queen Solalé's guards.

The queen's gaze lowers from the sunset's artistry to her own hands, her upturned palms pale against her otherwise russet skin. Energy seems to teem from every line and crease, like webs of lightning, shooting from her hands to her temples in a never-ceasing headache.

Her power, leaving her again to sustain the mortals—mortals who would kill her without hesitation if she ever lost control.

Even for a single hour.

She lowers her face into her hands, long fingernails pressing her skin. Streams of maroon hair fall over her shoulders, hiding her face from the eyes of her onlookers.

Only amongst her trusted court attendants and guards could she display such exhaustion. The rest of the kingdom can't know how weary she is. They must always see her as what she claims. A Radiant, stepped down from the Elysium. An immortal.

Not *this*.

"My lady?"

Queen Solalé lifts her gaze, meeting the guard's wide eyes. "Speak."

The man ducks his head in a noticeably hard swallow. "The Watchman."

The words crack through the grand court like land splitting beneath one's feet. Every pulse, every pain flees Queen Solalé's body. *The Watchman.*

The tree.

Layers of silk and lace stretch to the floor as she stands. "Send the petitioners away."

Her order turns the heels of the guards flanking the double doors to the yard. A line likely still waits outside for her attention. People who have waited all day.

But she's waited a century to hear those words.

The Watchman.

With a wordless nod to her Lord Chancellor, she steps down the wide stairs of her dais, the long train of her gown hissing behind her. She gathers the fabric, hoisting it to lengthen her strides. Her haste won't serve her image any better than her previous display of distress, but what does she care?

The tree.

Her heels click like a clock rigged for double-time as she races down hall after elegant hall. Hung paintings of herself as she once was watch her from both sides. Such strength. Such power. Such beauty.

All covering the rancid desperation of a slave dying without her master.

But not for much longer, she assures herself as she reaches the grand doors to what once was the Luminors' sanctum. Carved branches cover the white oak panels, a foreshadowing of what the doors hide. Will it be lit? Or has her hope caused her to misjudge the reason for her summoning altogether?

The guards need no command besides the pierce of her crystalline gaze to obey. They push the doors wide, and the queen fills her lungs, stretching the seams of her tight corset.

Light.

Brilliant gold and white rays. They radiate inside the massive white oak tree, as if a sun were trapped inside its long and sturdy, eternal branches.

Her jeweled hand covers her lips as she walks in. Slowly, slower. Stopping just before the incredible oak.

At last.

"Your Majesty?" the Watchman asks, his presence shadowed by the tree's glory.

The queen lowers her hand, letting the Watchman see the fullness of her joy. "Has their face appeared?"

The Watchman, the youngest of her sentinels, nods, waving his arm toward *The Book of Illuminance* resting upon a gold pedestal.

Queen Solalé's ears ring as she approaches it, eyes blurring with relief. She blinks them clear as she reaches the splayed book.

And there, spread across a new page, lays the image of a young man. Tan with dark hair, a look in his gaze so intense that she feels his presence as though he stood right behind her, watching.

Her smile flickers.

There he is. The new Illuminarch.

The one who will set my master free.

ACKNOWLEDGEMENTS

I foremost want to thank my Creator, Savior, Lord, and most loyal friend, Jesus Christ. I've written many words in my life, but not until I acknowledged You as my source and laid my gifts and dreams at Your feet did I find a story worth telling–a story that was more to *me* than just a clever idea with well-woven words, but a story that changed my life.

Secondly, I want to thank my husband, Rob. Your unwavering support and sacrifices of time, money, and energy (and possibly sanity at times!) for this dream of mine mean more to me than I know how to express. Thank you for letting me ramble for hours (days?) as I worked through this story, for reading *every single version* (I've lost count), for encouraging me when I felt incapable, and for all the ideas you gave me when my well ran dry.

I also want to thank my incredible family (especially my mom and my sister, Ashley), friends, and beta readers who have helped and encouraged me along the way. Your belief in me–even when I lost faith in myself–and bravery to support my dreams means the world to me. Thank you for being there in the many ways I needed through this process!

Also, a big shoutout to my publishing team! Jenna, my critique partner, thank you for listening to my long Marco Polos, helping me sort through all my ideas, and being a stable source of support and practical wisdom though the process. Olivia, thank you for being one of the loudest voices of encouragement for me, for all the gorgeous artwork you've done for my stories, and for all the unseen ways you supported this dream. Benita, my book designer, thank you for bringing your incredible skills and passion to the table and being an absolute delight to work alongside! Hannah, my line editor, thank you for your enthusiasm and love for this book and helping me polish it! Brigitte, my proofreader, thank you for believing in this story in such a deep way and for going above and beyond as a beta reader and later as a proofreader. They say it takes a village to raise a child, and a book is honestly no different. Thank you all so much!

And lastly, a huge thank you to everyone who contributed to my Kickstarter. Your financial investment is what made this book possible, and I am still stunned that you would make the sacrifice you did to see it brought to life. May God bless you in your giving and return it to you sevenfold!

KICKSTARTER SUPPORTERS

I would like to extend a special thanks to Kristee and Mark Preudhomme, my Ultimate Patrons, whose generous support on Kickstarter single-handedly covered the basic production costs of this book. Not only that, but these two have supported my family in so many other ways that helped me maintain sanity through the writing process as a stay-at-home, working mama of two little ones! Thank you, Kristee and Mark, for *everything* you've done to help me. You have truly helped me feel seen and loved by the Lord in this wild season.

Abigail Hathaway, Amy Shaw, Annette Scheible, Annie, Aslan's Compass, Bethel St., Breana Johnson, Breanna Swenson, Brigitte Cromey, Britt Sacrey, Candy Smith, Charity King, Christina Thomas Gonzales, Crystal Nicole, David DeHaan, David Lincoln, Dmytro Kocherhan, E.A. Hendryx, Emma Bahnmiller, Eric P., Erin McFarland, Gabriella, Giulia Santucci, Hannah Gaudette, Hannah McComis, Heather Griffin, Holly Morgan, Jenna Morgan, John W. Otte, JT Harris, Judith Parra, Justin Burgess, K Hendrick, Kaori Keiroz, Katie S., Katherine Malloy, Katrina Goforth, Kristen Bazen, Lale, Laurel Burgess, LJF, Mandy Inkrote, McKenna Hubbard, Melissa Ring, Megan Caudhill, Melody F. Barney, Michelle and Perry Swenson, Morgan G., Moriah Baldwin, Natalie Colburn, Noah Becchio, Noel Young, Pamela Hart, Rachael Ritchey, Rachel Rohde, Richard Lalchan, Ronda Lincoln-LaFleur, Samantha Mendell, Sarah Danielle, S.L. Klein, Sharon Price, Stephanie Cotta, Susan Rackley, Tania, Tiffany Sierra, Tom Belanger, Val Melvis

ABOUT THE AUTHOR

A.M. Daylin is a wife, mother of two young girls, and a follower of Jesus Christ. She has a deep passion for connecting with others' hearts through the power of stories and hopes that her words will help others experience healing as they go on thought-provoking, imaginative adventures. When not writing (or daydreaming about writing), you can find her drawing past her bedtime, hanging out with her family and Jesus, going for long drives whilst blasting cinematic music (that's normal, right?), obsessing over social media aesthetics (hey, it's part of her job!), and occasionally writing a song or two. She and her family currently live in Arizona, which inspired the setting for her debut. Connect with her on Instagram (@a.m.daylin) or at amdaylin.com.